HOLE LOTTA MAGIC

MAGICAL MIDWAY PARANORMAL COZY SERIES
BOOK SEVEN

LEANNE LEEDS

BADCHEN PUBLISHING

Hole Lotta Magic
ISBN Paperback: 978-1-950505-14-2
Published by Badchen Publishing
14125 W State Highway 29
Suite B-203 119
Liberty Hill, TX 78642 USA

Copyright © 2019 by Leanne Leeds

For permissions contact: info@badchenpublishing.com

Hole Lotta Magic
Published by Badchen Publishing
14125 W State Highway 29
Suite B-203 119
Liberty Hill, TX 78642 USA

HOLE LOTTA MAGIC

CHAPTER 1

"How did this happen?" I pressed, for what seemed like the hundredth time. Ethel Elkins sat serenely on the couch, knitting and humming. As if she didn't have a care in the world.

As if my cat wasn't just *stolen by a crazy person.*

"Charlotte—"

"Devana, I swear if you try to make excuses for her, I will completely blow my stack and eject you both," I snapped. I paced back and forth. The elegant witch nodded once, but she didn't remove her hand from Ethel's shoulder. "How does the guardian of the Magical Midway get kidnapped *in a Fendi bag?* With a room full of witches? How did *you* not know?" I glared at the old woman.

Ever since Ethel Elkins arrived, she'd declared herself as all-knowing and omnipotent.

Which was odd considering things kept happening to us that weren't good.

"Charlotte, how did *you* not know?" Tabitha asked me calmly. "How did *I* not know my mother was behind my capture? Or that my best friend was a witch? Dating a gay guy and lying to me? No one's infallible, Charlotte, and yelling at the nice old woman will not get your cat back."

"Nice old woman," I snorted and glared at the angelic-looking Ethel Elkins as she knitted, smiled, and hummed. It was the calmest I had ever seen the old norn, come to think of it. My eyes tightened as her humming grew louder. "If I can rubber band back here, why can't Samson? Ms. Elkins?"

The old woman ignored me.

"I think you hurt her feelings," Gunther said.

"That woman doesn't have feelings," the bright ghost of Gunther's father snorted behind him as he entered the yurt. Gunther's mother, also a spirit, tsk-tsked him but he continued scowling at the old woman. My parents, coming in behind them, watched with concerned faces. "She's got a steely heart encased in a stone chest, that one."

Ethel Elkins stopped her weaving and her

humming. Her eyes lifted from the sparkling yarn to glare at Roland Makepeace. One eyebrow shot up. "Takes one to know one, tubby. Devana, locate the cat," Ethel Elkins waved dismissively.

Devana, the graceful and deadly huntress witch, bowed and turned to head back to their room.

I blinked. "It's that easy?"

"Finding him? Yes, it's that easy," Ms. Elkins nodded. "She's a huntress witch. What the heck did you think I kept her around for? Her sparkling personality? She can find *anything*. You just seem to ignore that, and you don't ask her. Your human propensity to discount magical tools in favor of...whatever that plodding thing is that you do—"

"Logic? And that was kind of rude," I complained.

"No ruder than you all have been since Devana helped Roland," Ms. Elkins said. She set aside her wool and rocked to push her round, short body off the couch. Gunther leaned forward and reached out his arm. "Thank you, boy," she humphed.

"Ms. Elkins—" I started.

"She'll find him, but *getting* him? That's another story." Ms. Elkins drifted toward the kitchenette. "That human can't *really* steal the Magical Midway power; there's no human magic left in the human world that would let a mere mortal do that. And she can't kill him, either."

I exhaled noisily. "Well, that's a relief—"

"Not without paranormal world support," Ms. Elkins cut me off.

"The Council could assist her, Charlotte," my mother said. We all followed the old woman toward the teapot. "They can't come onto the grounds and steal Samson, but they could get a human to do it *for* them if they chose to."

"And Samson wouldn't fear a mortal," my father continued.

"Nor could the cat defend himself," Roland pointed out. "Not against a human."

"Why not?" I asked.

"The oath, Charlotte." Gunther waved his hands in a circle. "The one you require of the paranormals you admit into the circus."

"We are all bound to an oath never to harm a human," Fiona said. "I imagine that applies to Samson."

"Yeah, but that's just a pledge, right?" I gestured to Fiona.

She shook her head. "No, friend, nothing in

our world is *just* a pledge. It is an oath, and broken oaths have repercussions."

"If we broke our oath, it would destroy us, Charlotte," Ningul chimed in and draped his arm around Fiona. "It is, actually, a spell we put on ourselves. We acknowledge that death is welcome if we so much as harm a hair on a human's head that visits here. It has been that way for years, maybe from the beginning."

"It is a strong enchantment. Some creatures here can be dangerous, child," Roland reminded me.

"I know that," I snapped, irritated. I thought the days of discovering something was super-serious, something I probably should have known, were over. Apparently, there were still mysteries about my circus and my world that my gaggle of paranormal assistants hadn't bothered to tell me.

Our world is made of mysteries, Gunther thought.

"Can I have Jeannie grant a wish to bring him back?" I turned to Uncle Phil. "Would she do that? It wouldn't even matter where he was, right?"

Uncle Phil was the third and final ghost participating in the discussion—though you wouldn't know it. He looked as mortal as anyone else in the room. Well. Anyone else in the room not a ghost. His girlfriend, Jeannie, granted his wish to have his body back. Though I believed the djinn granted his request as much for *herself* as for him.

"We could ask her," he shrugged. "I'll be right back."

"This would be the first issue we solved in record time, right?" Gunther said as he smiled.

"It would be nice to resolve something fast for a change," I nodded, hopeful.

"You could solve everything quickly if you relied on magic instead of whatever human nonsense you get on with," Ms. Elkins told me.

"If I'd used magic or Devana to find Tabitha…" I said, but I trailed off. Ethel Elkins was right in some ways. I could have checked with Cama, the death bat, to see if Tabitha was alive when she was missing, and I didn't. I probably could have used something else to find her, and I didn't. Gunther, Aidan, Kyle, and I had hit the streets looking for information.

The truth was the longer I was ringmaster, the less I trusted the magical world. I hadn't told anyone that, but it was how I felt deep down.

The super-powered goddess Maggie, her counterpart Eiggam, thousand-year-old grievances. It all seemed to obscure people's motivations. Motivations that magic could hide but that good old-fashioned human nosiness *usually* uncovered.

I trusted Uncle Phil's girlfriend, Jeannie, though, and I believed that she would grant my wish for Samson to return home.

I believed that right up until Uncle Phil's voice shouted Jeannie's name from across the Magical Midway.

A pile of glitter in the center of her food cart was all that remained of Jeannie.

"*That's* your uncle's girlfriend?" Tabitha asked as she craned her neck to see around Gunther. Bob leaned down to inspect the multi-colored sparkle. "You know, I read about this when I was looking for you, but I *didn't* believe it. You really do turn people into a pile of glitter. That's *bizarre.*"

"Anyone paranormal that passes away on the fairgrounds turns into glitter," I leaned close to her and spoke in a low voice. "We never want to draw awareness to what we really are, and we can't let the humans get a hold of a deceased paranormal. So this was the enchantment one of my forefathers came up with. Nothing left to freak anyone out."

"But how do you know what happened to her?"

"Her ghost has to be around here somewhere," I turned around and scanned for the incorporeal Jeannie.

"She is a djinn, Charlotte," Uncle Phil said in a low voice thick with grief. "They have no souls. If she still exists, it is in a realm that witches cannot reach. We will never speak to her again. She is truly, *truly* gone."

"I'm so sorry, Uncle Phil," I whispered. He nodded without glancing up.

We all looked at the pile of glitter that had been Jeannie.

"I still can't believe you turn people into glitter," Tabitha mumbled as Bob, the lares guard, put his arm around her. "I mean...*glitter?*"

"We just explained how this works. And why," I told Tabitha, annoyance creeping into my tone. Before things escalated, I turned to the lares security guard. "I know we preoccupied your normal patrol with Samson's kidnapping, but did you all see anything?"

"My brother Gallus patrolled near here

tonight," Bob answered, looking at Uncle Phil and the sparkly remains of my uncle's companion with unease. "I can get him and bring him here. I guess you will want to question him."

Bob's about-face from jovial cut-up to severe Roman guardian always surprised me. If there was ever a night to be serious, however, tonight was probably it. In the space of two hours, Samson had been snatched, and Jeannie had died. Since she was a djinn, the probability of death by natural causes was so low it wasn't even worth contemplating.

I nodded, and he left to find his monosyllabic brother.

"Who would want to kill Jeannie?" Fiona asked me from the back of the food stand. "She never had a cross word to say to anyone."

"No, but she was one of the few djinns left in the paranormal world anywhere," Uncle Phil said as he rose. "And she could have returned Samson to us in the flutter of an eye if she wished to. Perhaps someone didn't want us to have that option."

"A human couldn't kill a djinn, Uncle Phil," I pointed out. "Whatever Tabitha's mom is working to become? Mrs. Stevens is *still* human."

"Maybe she *is* working with the Witches' Council," Fiona suggested.

"There is no way. I would've known," Tabitha disagreed.

"The same way you knew your mother plotted your kidnapping and was trying to take down your ex-best friend?" Fiona snapped. She thrust herself off the wall of the small enclosure and leaned toward Tabitha, her eyes narrowing. "I don't think you get a vote on what's possible and impossible here, *human*."

"Everyone just calm down," I said to the group while glancing at Fiona. "We've got about ten people piled in here, it's getting hot, and everybody is stressed out. I'm stressed out. Let's not turn on each other."

"When did *she* become part of *us*?" Fiona asked me, pointing at Tabitha. I noticed Anya standing just behind Fiona and Ningul. She was curiously silent but stared at Tabitha warily.

"You and I can talk about this *alone*," I said as I jerked my head toward the gathered throng. Fiona gave me a cocky wave of her hand and rolled her eyes.

The residents of the Magical Midway realized that something had taken place. Faces peered in through the open service window of the tiny food stand. Panicked whispers echoed into the room as one person shared with a new person, and then that person explained to yet another person standing next to them. Within thirty seconds, questions began as fear sizzled in the air.

"Now Jeannie is dead!"

"Samson is gone, and now Jeannie's been murdered!"

"Oh no, oh no, what are we to do? What's to become of us?"

"Someone's killing us one by one!"

"It's the Witches' Council, I'm telling you!"

"The humans took the cat! If they could take the cat, why couldn't they kill a djinn! They're growing more powerful—"

"And smarter!"

"And meaner!"

"We have to get out of here! Can we go where the Makepeace Circus—"

"Yeah, how come *they're* safe?"

"Maybe it's that Makepeace boy that did it!"

"Maybe he left us out here to be picked off one by one!"

I closed the open sliding window, but that only dampened the shrieks. Fiona and Ningul, Anya, Uncle Phil, Tabitha, Gunther and I stared at one another in silence as we awaited Bob's return.

As the back door opened, I noticed Anya had positioned herself behind Tabitha. Her hand rested on the knife at her hip.

Great.

CHAPTER 2

"Samson is in the human town of Mickwac, and he's on the move," Devana told Kyle, Aidan, Gunther and me once we were back in the yurt. Anya and Fiona were across the room whispering frantically to one another. My parents and Gunther's parents remained behind to take care of Uncle Phil. He insisted that he and he alone would gather Jeanie's sparkly remains up for her interment.

Ms. Elkins continued humming on the couch, her muumuu fanned out around her as she knitted.

"That's not very useful," Kyle said and crisscrossed his arms. The former detective shifted his head. "I could have worked out there was a fifty percent chance someone took the cat to Mickwac, an even bigger percentage chance if I knew that Tabitha's mother had catnapped him."

"I *apologize* for not speaking more quickly. I did not intend to motivate you to cut me off due to an ill-timed pause, Mr. Roberts," Devana told him serenely, her head bowed. Raising her eyes, she met Kyle's harsh gaze. "Perhaps if I had spoken faster, you would have learned the additional information that would have been contained in the latter half of my statement." Devana paused and stared.

Clearly, Devana had had just about enough of Kyle treating her like a felon that escaped punishment. The centaur was new to the paranormal world, but his sense of justice held him rigid even in the face of magic and prophecies. Devana's poisoning of Gunther's father was necessary, Ms. Elkins claimed, but Kyle didn't buy it—and it showed every time he talked to her.

"Sorry, did I hurt your feelings?" Kyle sneered. Aidan reached out and laid a tender hand on his boyfriend's shoulder. "Do you even *have* them? Feelings, I mean?"

Aidan removed his hand and exhaled.

"You have been a centaur and a paranormal

for all the time it would take the Goddess to flutter an eye compared to me, Mr. Roberts. Talk to me anew in a hundred years, in two hundred years, when the weight of your people and all that they have done lands on your shoulders to remedy." Devana strode forward and tilted her head to peer even more intensely into the centaur's angry gaze. "My sister Mina has damaged the balance of the world by her actions, and even now may be part of the peril of Samson and the death of the djinn—"

"Even more reason you shouldn't be here!" Kyle raised his voice.

"I am the only one who fully appreciates what we face," Devana stepped forward again, her eyes narrowing and her skin glowing faintly. "I am not a Huntress because I want to be, Mr. Roberts. I am a Huntress because sometimes sacrifices are required for the whole to remain. You were a human police officer, you should respect that truth."

"What have *you* sacrificed? Charlotte gives you a bed to sleep in—"

"I have no mother, no father, no husband, no child, no familiar, no *tribe*." Devana's eyes brimmed with tears, her voice filled with emotion. "I am obligated to carry out choices that rend my spirit into pieces, and I must trust the norn when she advises me I must murder."

Gunther and I clasped hands as we stood beside Devana. We all had been uncomfortable and alarmed by Devana's attempted murder of Roland Makepeace, but Roland Makepeace *himself* had absolved her. His death reunited him with the love of his life, Gerda—and that was a gift he was grateful for. Frankly, when Roland was alive? He seemed miserable without her.

"You *have* a tribe," I declared with a faint smile. "You live here with us. Though we don't understand why you do what you do sometimes, no one in this room could say that Roland Makepeace's death caused—" I paused, searching for the words.

"What Charlotte means is his afterlife seems much more fulfilling than his life was," Gunther finished for me. "My father was a fierce man in life, bitter and resentful over the loss of my mother. Kyle, you will have to let your judgment go at some point. My mother and my father are *thankful* to Devana for what she did."

"It was unavoidable, anyway," I continued. "Roland seemed to pass on to the next life just fine as soon as he set eyes on Gerda, without Devana's help."

"You have a sincere sense of justice, my friend," Gunther smiled at Kyle. "You just may need to partner it with some understanding. These are complex times."

Aidan remained silent, his eyes bleak. Kyle looked unconvinced by our words.

"If you want to suspect someone, how about that new human?" Anya asked. She and Fiona walked over to us.

"Keep your voice down, she'll hear you," I peered into the main room.

"No, she won't." Fiona cocked her head. "She didn't return with us to the yurt. Perhaps because she didn't want to answer questions about where she was when Jeannie died."

"Fiona and I think the human killed the djinn." Anya balled her fists.

"I mean, seriously—how many times can someone comment on a pile of glitter?" Fiona asked. "She was pushing off suspicion, I know it. Pretending she was surprised to see it."

"She and her mother being against one another? *Anyone* could have seen through that." Anya rolled her eyes. "Misdirection."

"Lies, she means." Fiona's eyes flashed.

"I *know* what *misdirection* means," I snapped, and wiped my eyes. When I opened them back up, the two mean girls were still staring at me with expectation.

~

"Before we proceed," Devana said after we all sat down again, "I would like to stress that although Samson cannot be *killed* by a human, he can suffer. Not eating or drinking, even for a guardian, would be miserable."

"Especially for *that* guardian," Fiona murmured.

"And if the Witches' Council is in league with that woman or the girl…" Ms. Elkins set aside her needles and yarn. "The longer they have him? The more magical attacks they can try. We may be sure humans can't kill Samson, but that doesn't mean the wicked triplets couldn't figure out a way to break his tie to the Magical Midway."

"And your lawgiver powers may be ineffective here." Aidan spoke softly. I shifted to study my friend and realized he appeared tired. His hair was disheveled, his shirt rumpled. There were lines beneath his eyes. "You cannot freeze humans."

"Yes, I can!"

"When Tiffany Drake was murdered,

Charlotte froze…" Gunther's comment trailed off.

"I *didn't*, though, did I?" I muttered as I thought back to our initial visit to Mickwac—the one where a mobster's daughter was assassinated in my parents' animal shelter by Hayden. "I thought about freezing both Michael Hayden *and* Anthony Drake, but I didn't because we couldn't explain it to Melissa Hayden."

"You don't think it's strange that your old best friend is best buddies with the sister of the *new* town mobster?" Fiona leaned back in a chair and crossed her arms.

"Melissa Hayden isn't anything like—"

"Charlotte Astley, I am *baffled* by you, sister," Anya leaned forward and smashed the palms of her hands down on her thighs. Pointing across the coffee table, she shook her finger at me. "You are a *witch* and a *ringmaster witch* at that! Someone has taken your familiar, your guardian catnapped! Killed your uncle's paramour! Where is your anger? Your fury? Your thirst for *vengeance*?"

"We are not at *war*, naiad," Devana said, stepping around the couch from behind Ms. Elkins. "We are a magical circus, containing untold power. Charlotte has the abilities she does and Samson the defenses he does because this will ever be a target. So long as it endures. This is not an outlier. This should be expected."

"Especially considering your boyfriend has hidden his circus away from everyone, and we're waving out in the open with a bullseye on our yurt," Fiona snapped, and scowled at Gunther.

Why is everyone mad at me suddenly? I asked Gunther telepathically.

They are just fearful, Charlotte, Gunther replied. *You and Samson are the two beings they count on to look after them, to protect them from everything outside this magical dome. With Samson gone, they're frightened. Even if they don't want to admit it. I suspect it's not pleasant to be reminded that the Witches' Council is held at bay by you and the snarky cat.*

"Whatever else is going on here, we still have a responsibility to the paranormal world to keep it hidden from the humans," I told Fiona. "Gunther's circus hides in the place of power so it can protect them while he's here with us. Remember, they don't *have* a guardian."

"Well, now *we* don't have a guardian, so why are *we* still here?" Anya asked.

They had a point.

I could sense the uneasy anxiety gathering like a rising flood within the circus. The

Magical Midway was my home, and I hadn't considered moving it to the space between worlds *because* it was my home. I preferred it where I was.

That, and I still hoped that Samson could rubber band himself back onto the fairgrounds. People kept being wrong about what I could and couldn't do. Maybe they were wrong about Samson, too.

Though if they were, he probably would've been here by now.

I groaned.

"Okay, here's what we're going to do," I said as I stood up. "I will send the Magical Midway to the place of power with the Makepeace Circus. That should make everyone feel a little safer while we figure out what's going on."

"I *don't* want to go there!" Ms. Elkins protested. She jolted her large body up off the couch so she could argue more effectively.

"Ms. Elkins, you can see what's coming, so I want you to go with them." Her eyes bugged out, and she opened her mouth to argue, but I waved my hand in her direction to silence her.

My excuse for leaving her was that the norn's knowledge of future events would be of more use to Anya and Fiona—though truthfully, I just wanted her out of the way. The old lady's farseeing hadn't helped out with Samson at all.

Or Jeannie.

And I did not want to run around Mickwac with *Ms. Elkins*. No way.

"Devana, you will come with us."

"Who's us?" Anya asked.

"Aidan, Kyle, Gunther, and me." I gestured to Fiona and Anya. Anya's cheeks burned as red as her stubbled short hair. "I know you probably prefer to come, but right now you guys are way too hyped up to be of any use."

"Hey, now wait—" Fiona leaned forward.

"Gunther has witch skills I don't, and I need him with me," I cut her off before she could argue. "Devana is a huntress. Kyle used to be a detective, and Aidan knows this town. Actually, Aidan? Go see if you can find Fortuna. Let's bring her, too. She's a strong mind reader, and she's familiar with the human world."

"I'm familiar with the human world!" Anya protested.

"You're not. You *assume* you are, but you're not. Not in the way we are. Besides, I need you both here," I explained to the indignant water nymph. "Jeannie's murder took place *here*. Samson's kidnapping happened *here*. I can't be in two places at once, and someone in the circus saw something."

"Or *did* something," Fiona added, turning to Anya. I nodded.

"We have to look for Samson, and Samson is definitely not here. The information we need to get him back, though, *may* be here. I need you guys to talk to people. Hold this place together. Uncle Phil will be useless for a while," I reminded them. Anya and Fiona both nodded, the lines on their tense faces softening now that I had given them a role to play.

"What about the human?" Fiona demanded. She spat the word human like it coated her mouth in spoiled milk.

"She's coming with us," I told her.

Fiona glared at me.

"Look, I get that you don't know her and that this all seems...suspicious."

"It doesn't *seem* suspicious, Charlotte," Fiona said firmly. "It *is* suspicious."

"You don't know Tabitha, but I *do*. In fact, I don't think I've ever known anyone more honest than Tabitha. I don't believe that she's capable of being in league with her mother—"

"I did not know that my mother would take Charlotte's cat," Tabitha said, striding into the yurt, Bob firmly behind her. Gallus, his brother, clinked in after him, wrapped in Roman armor.

Fiona and Anya stared at her.

"If I had, I would have told Charlotte. I would have stopped it."

"Excuse us if we don't *fully* trust that, human," Fiona replied.

"I have a name. I'm not just a *human*," Tabitha responded readily.

"Your kind shouldn't be welcome here," Anya said, pointing at Tabitha.

Fortuna, who had just come in, gawked at Anya from the door, disturbed.

•

CHAPTER 3

IT DIDN'T SURPRISE ME WHEN BOB STOOD BESIDE us as I sent the Magical Midway to the other realm. The lares guards were specifically guards of a *place*, and that place was the Magical Midway. So it probably should have.

Since Tabitha showed up, though? Bob had been stuck to her like glue.

Once the Midway was safe, we made our way to the vehicles in my parents' animal shelter parking lot. Bob jumped in the back seat of the truck and slid next to Tabitha.

I felt like I should say something, but I figured somewhere within his brain, Bob had determined that the Magical Midway guardian being kidnapped justified his leaving the grounds. He wasn't entirely wrong.

I suspected, though, that Bob's attraction to Tabitha had as much to do with the choice as Samson.

Devana climbed all the way in the back and remained silent the entire ride. It was as if the huntress wasn't even in the car.

"So, are you Charlotte's personal bodyguard?" Tabitha asked the moon-eyed Bob as she turned from the window.

Samson, can you hear me? I called out mentally as we pulled into the road.

"I am the protector of the magical circus, ma'am," Bob answered her respectfully. I heard him shift in the back seat. "My job, my entire *purpose*, really, is to ensure that the Magical Midway is protected from any threat. That it...endures."

I glanced into the rearview mirror again, surprised at Bob's seriousness as he faced Tabitha. His voice had deepened from the silly joviality that usually emanated from him. A featherbrained fog typically extended out at least ten feet around the lares.

Yet with Tabitha? It was gone. He was really into her.

Love can change people, Gunther thought.

Love doesn't change people, I thought back as we gained speed on the highway. *Love just makes people more who they always were, I think.*

Perhaps, he responded.

Samson, can you hear me? Where are you?

Silence.

"What is it?" Tabitha asked, interrupting Bob and his description of what door mice tasted like in Roman times.

Dormice, Gunther thought. *It was actually food for the wealthy in his time, believe it or not.*

Thanks, but no thanks.

"Nothing, Tabitha, I'm just thinking," I told her, glancing at her in the mirror.

"What are you thinking about?" she asked me. Bob frowned as Tabitha turned her attention away from him. As if sensing his unhappiness, she turned back, gave him a broad smile, and patted his hand. The frown disappeared.

"Door mice," Gunther told my friend.

Samson? Samson, come on, dude! Not a time to keep your thoughts to yourself.

I was sure that as we traveled closer to the town I would be able to hear some echo of Samson's thoughts, but there was nothing. Just a bereft silence that felt vast and wide.

It was frightening to be so cut off from the cat. Our bond was strong, intensely strong. What could be interfering with our telepathic connection?

Samson! Answer me!

I hoped Fortuna was having better luck with her telepathic skills than I was having with mine. Clearly my supernatural abilities, once again, dropped to almost nothing when we stepped off the fairgrounds.

"No, she's not thinking about dormice," Tabitha told Gunther. Her finger made circles in the air, her index finger pointed at my head. "If I still know Charlotte, I bet she's obsessing over her lost cat. And doubting herself."

"Tabitha, he's not just a cat. He's…Never mind, just let me think," I warned her and my foot dropped deeper into the accelerator.

"Charlotte doesn't like being called out," Tabitha confided to Gunther and Bob, her hand blocking the outrageously loud whisper from the driver's seat as if she meant for me not to hear. Even though she did. With a nod, she slapped against the back of my seat as my jaw tightened.

"I don't like being messed with when my cat

has been kidnapped, that's all," I snapped, my fingers growing tight around the steering wheel. "So if you're going to start messing with me to distract yourself from the fact that your parents are lunatics, just don't. Go back to flirting with Bob."

"He's flirting with *me*, actually," Tabitha pointed out. Bob blushed profusely and stammered.

"I'm so sorry—"

"Hey, Bob, chill out," Tabitha told him. "I didn't say I disliked you flirting with me." Bob beamed. Tabitha rolled her eyes.

I did my best not to gag.

"How did you *not* clue in to the fact that your mother was working with Raven at the coven?" I asked Tabitha in an attempt to bring the conversation back to the immediate threat. "They would've had to spend some time together plotting to get you in that cave, wouldn't they? And how does your father play in all this?"

"I would think so," Tabitha said as she sat back against the seat and crossed her arms. "I don't know when they would've had the time, though. Raven's always had this weird thing for me. My mother, too, oddly enough," she said. I could hear her fingers tapping against the chrome on the back door. It made a tinny clink-clink-clink sound that fell silent just before it got annoying. "I can't recall my father and Raven *ever* being civil to one another in public, honestly."

Samson, can you hear me? Samson!

"Sometimes we don't notice things we think we should," Gunther said in a tone of voice that implied he thought I should be noticing something.

"What's *that* supposed to mean?" I asked him.

"Doesn't mean anything, Charlotte. It was just an observation," Gunther told me without pulling his gaze from the window. "It seems to me that we overlook things we don't want to see much more often than is good for us."

"Your boyfriend's a philosopher," Tabitha observed with some amusement.

"Or he's depressed because nothing seems to go right for us," I snapped at her.

As the last of my rapid-fire statement left my lips, I felt a flash of guilt. I had a bad habit of taking my stress out on the people around me, and I knew that my frustration was not entirely Tabitha's fault.

Unless Fiona and Anya were right. But they couldn't be right.

"Charlotte's right, though I wouldn't have put

it in quite those terms. I'm just feeling a bit melancholy, that's all," Gunther told Tabitha.

"Well, quit it," I told him. "We don't have time for feelings right now."

Gunther's eyes met mine. He didn't respond.

"Is there anyone in this car you're not annoyed with, Charlotte?" Tabitha asked with some amusement. "Still snippy when you're stressed out, I see."

"I'm not annoyed at everyone," I told her. "Not annoyed with Gunther, not annoyed with Bob—"

"Thanks, boss," he answered cheerfully.

"Don't mention it."

"I already did. Mention it, I mean. So, I guess I'm retroactively sorry for mentioning it. I didn't know you were going to tell me not to mention it."

"You're a real hoot, you know that?" Tabitha laughed.

"Oh yeah, he's hysterical," I muttered.

The five of us continued our steady progress toward the town, joining Devana in her silence. Our first stop?

Tabitha's parents' house.

~

"Weird," Tabitha said when we pulled up in front of the house. "I haven't been here for ages. It all looks the same, and yet it all feels so different." Without any grandiose movement, Bob slid closer to Tabitha. His shoulders were arched and tense as he silently scanned the dark windows of the house for signs of a threat.

Samson, can you hear me? We're at the Stevenses' house. Are you there? Samson, please answer me.

We all slid out of the car and stood in the driveway staring at the house as if waiting for it to give up its secrets. After a few seconds, Tabitha broke the silence.

"If I were going to suggest a place to start? Back there," Tabitha pointed toward the towering iron fence and walked toward it. "There's a storage room in the back around this way. If someone is doing some kind of black magic hoodoo voodoo thing with your magic cat, it would probably be back there. It's the only place someone could hide something from the maids, and Mom has her ritual room in it."

"Let's go, then," I said and followed Tabitha toward the gate.

"We should wait for the rest of the group." Gunther reached forward to grab my shoulder. I ducked his hand and continued walking. "Charlotte!"

"What?" I asked without turning around. Tabitha's gaze swung back toward me, and she raised her eyebrow. Bob remained silent beside her, matching her pace step for step, but his expression clearly denoted his discomfort with our advance. "Samson could be *right back there*, and the longer we wait, the more danger he could be in."

"I understand, but we should wait," Gunther said quietly.

"The guardian is not here," Devana said quietly.

"Not for nothing, Devana, but I'm still going to check." I kept walking. There wasn't time to stop and wait for Kyle and Aidan. Or Fortuna. Or to leave just because Devana made a pronouncement.

I didn't want to wait, I didn't want to talk about it, I didn't want to rely on other people telling me I was wrong. I needed to act—I needed to find that stupid, frustrating, aggravating cat and keep him from getting—

"Charlotte, I know you're worried, but please," Gunther told me as he stepped closer. His voice was low but clear. "Kyle is a police officer in this world, a human lawgiver—and he'll be an important asset if things go sideways here. I'm not asking you to stop, I'm just asking you to slow—"

"Kyle's not human, he's a centaur," I snapped at Gunther, turning to confront him. "And he's not a lawgiver, we are! And this isn't a human problem, this is a paranormal problem—"

"Our lawgiver powers won't work on humans," Gunther reminded me. "Your offensive powers are useless here, and mine are greatly diminished by the distance. All we have is Bob and—"

Gunther's characterization of my powers as useless stung.

"Mine are not," Devana said quietly. "I am as deadly here as I am anywhere."

Gunther glanced at her.

"I will protect you all," Bob said seriously, his eyes shining with confidence. "It is what I do, Gunther. It's who I am."

"You do realize that part of being who you are means that you have confidence in a fight even when you shouldn't, right?" Gunther asked him with a half-smile. Bob's eyebrows rose, and his gaze fell. "I'm not trying to insult you, Bob, I'm just saying that we don't know what we're walking into."

"You're not trying to insult *him*, but you're cool with calling me useless?" I asked my boyfriend. Gunther looked at me, his eyes blinking. Confusion flashed across his handsome face.

"I didn't call you—"

"You did. You certainly did."

"Man, you guys are a *lot* less together than I would have thought for people with the kind of powers you have," Tabitha said as she looked at us.

"You know, if *you* had been a little bit more together, maybe we wouldn't be here," I snapped. Tabitha's face remained impassive.

I was trying to push it down, I was trying not to blame, but I was angry at *everyone*. I was mad at Tabitha for trusting that lunatic Raven what's-his-face, at Tabitha's mother for introducing her to a coven, at Gunther for...at Gunther for...

"Love, I did not mean to insult you, not in any way," Gunther told me. Aidan, Kyle and Fortuna pulled up. "I apologize sincerely if I hurt you. The argument is over in any case. They have arrived."

"Great," I snapped.

"Charlotte, I love you, love you more than you

realize." Gunther pulled me into his arms. His lips pressed against my hair, and he whispered. "I support you always. I know that you are struggling to contain your emotions, and it's understandable. But it's clouding your judgment."

I pushed him away. "Was that your polite way of saying I'm too *emotional*?"

"Uh oh," Tabitha murmured.

"What happened?" Bob asked, confused.

"I don't know what the rules of engagement are in the paranormal world, but in the human world? Telling a woman she's too emotional is—"

"Insulting," I finished fiercely. I felt Gunther withdraw from my head.

"I'm sorry, that's not what I meant. I never intended an insult—"

"Your mother was killed. Your father died. We're always apart now. *None* of that makes you emotional? Really?" I asked him, my eyes narrowing.

"Charlotte, I—"

"Forget it," I seethed at my boyfriend. He stared back at me, his face flushed.

"Hey, what's going—" Kyle asked, but Aidan stopped him with a light hand and a slight nod. His eyes sparkled with the knowledge of the fight Gunther, and I had just had, and Fortuna looked concerned at the sparks of emotion she read from the two of us.

"Tabitha says that the back storage house is this way," I pointed to the gate on the side of the house. "We were just going to check it out."

"We were waiting for you three to check it out," Tabitha said as she turned to follow me.

"We weren't, though, Gunther and Charlotte were arguing about—" Bob's explanation was interrupted by Tabitha whacking him hard with a balled fist. Bob didn't even flinch as he straightened up and smiled at them. "We *were* waiting for you. She is absolutely right. Glad you could make it, ladies and gentleman."

CHAPTER 4

"THERE'S NOTHING HERE," TABITHA SAID WITH A shrug. "Devana was right. Wherever she took the cat, it wasn't here."

Sarah Stevens hadn't precisely created a serene place to get away from it all. If her home was modern, sleek, and minimalistic with everything in its place, this place was the opposite of that. It looked like a hoarder's version of Avalon Grove, the occult shop in town.

"I thought Samantha Goodfellow said your Mom hid her craft from your father?" I asked Tabitha as we rifled through the books, papers, and items piled up around us. "How did he not notice *this*?"

"Dad never came out here, at least not when I

was growing up," Tabitha said. She picked up an apothecary jar and peeked at it. Someone had filled it with pink jelly beans. Tabitha unsealed the transparent top and popped one in her mouth. "I don't know that I can really get across how little my father was here at the house."

"He was here when we came to talk to your parents," Aidan said, his voice gravelly. Gunther's eyes narrowed as he glanced at Aidan, and even though his spirit had withdrawn from my brain, I could sense his unease about my friend. "Came home while we were speaking to your mother..." Aidan's voice trailed off as if he had run out of strength.

"Well, I mean, he *lives* here," Tabitha said, flipping through a thick leather-bound book. "But he almost treats it like a hotel. He eats here. He sleeps here. He throws the occasional work party here. The rest of the time he's at the office."

"Is he having an affair with someone there?" Kyle asked without embarrassment as he looked up from examining an *Il Pirata* menu.

"Don't know," Tabitha shrugged. "Wouldn't surprise me. But it's not like he would tell me if he was."

Charlotte...

I froze, holding a brass container, listening as the shadow of Samson's call faded from my head.

"Samson, where are you?" I shouted mentally and verbally. The others dropped what they were doing and stared.

Charlotte...

"Samson, I can hear you. Where are you?"

Silence. I clutched the brass lamp so hard that my knuckles turned white. Listening intently, I picked up nothing more.

"He's gone," I told my friends as I put down the lamp. "He called my name twice and then nothing else. He sounded...I don't know, groggy? Tired?"

"Well, he's been snatched," Tabitha said. "Speaking from experience, just knowing that you're kidnapped is kind of tiring." Bob shifted closer to her and patted her shoulder consolingly.

"Or he's sedated," I said.

"You're guessing she gave him the scopolamine," Kyle said as he turned and swiveled his head around. "There's a small box of those patches here someplace. I *just* saw them." He walked into an alcove off the main room and poked around. Aidan leaned against a desk and watched his boyfriend glumly.

"The Devil's Breath," Devana said and shuddered.

"What?"

"The drug you keep speaking of, the one that Stevens used to manipulate the high priestess. We make it from the seeds of the borrachero tree that grows in South America. It has been used by our people for years for…different things," she said. She gave me a furtive glance. "We have known it as hell's bells, devil's trumpets, angel's trumpets, henbane, moonflowers, jimson weed. But now? It is most commonly called Devil's Breath. It eradicates free will."

"Wait—henbane?" I asked. Henbane was the herb that poisoned my Uncle Phil. Ningul told me that witches have a specific sensitivity to henbane.

"It doesn't *eliminate* free will," Kyle rolled his eyes. "Yes, it makes someone more *suggestible* if they're given a high enough dose—"

"It eliminates free will," Devana declared again, cutting him off. Kyle rolled his shoulders back and glared at the huntress witch, his eyes dark.

"I think we're all saying the same thing," Aidan said with a sigh.

"No, we are not," Devana said. Raising her

head, she stared at Kyle. "The centaur is speaking of cerebral effects, suggestibility. I am trying to explain to you that the magical properties of the Devil's Breath are profound, and in the right dosage and with the proper intent behind it, the seeds will erase the free will of the target. The plants are beautiful, enchanted...and destructive."

"Like you," Kyle sneered. Devana stared daggers at him.

"Enough, Kyle," I interjected before they could continue.

"Guys?" Fortuna stepped into the room. She held out a brown pod toward the huntress. "I found huge plastic bags of white powder next to these pods in the other room. Is this the Devil's Breath?" Devana leaned forward and nodded. "Take a look at this," Fortuna gestured for us to follow, and we all went through the archway to an adjoining room.

"Holy henbane," Gunther said as he breathed out.

"There's enough here to poison the entire Magical Midway," I said. We looked at the stacks upon stacks of blue and white bags crammed with powder, next to a large commercial grinder. Someone filled the corner of the place with hundreds of pods, the other corner the processed seeds.

"There might be enough here to poison the entire town of Mickwac," Kyle said.

"I guess my mother wasn't meditating in here like she claimed," Tabitha mumbled. She paused in the doorway, her eyes wide. "What could she possibly be aiming to do with all this?"

"You know, this looks like far more than just your mother planning to steal the Magical Midway's energy from me," I told Tabitha. "Amassing the *one* drug that paranormal witches are hypersensitive to?"

"Sensitive how?" Tabitha asked me.

"Uncle Phil was poisoned to death by henbane," I told her. "A nasty piece of work was trying to drug his girlfriend so she'd leave him alone, and Uncle Phil drank it by mistake. It wouldn't kill her because of what she was, but it killed him."

"So, this could be intended to control humans, large numbers of humans." Gunther rubbed his chin and peered at the blue and white bags. "It could also be intended to drug the Magical Midway into compliance, but not kill them."

"Or it could be the first attack in a witch civil war," I said, spinning to him.

"A witch civil war?" he asked. "Aren't we kind of in one already?"

"With the Witches' Council, sure," I acknowledged. "The human witches have been out of the whole thing." I pointed toward the mountains of powder. "Maybe not anymore."

The eight of us stared at Sarah Stevens's drug processing chamber.

"This isn't helping." I threw a book down in irritation. Looking up from a notebook she was flipping through, Tabitha studied me. "What?"

She laid down the book and grinned at me. "Can I talk to you outside?"

"Why not here?" I asked, glancing down at the desk and pulling up another sheaf of handwritten notes, and more *Il Pirata* menus.

"Please?" Tabitha asked with a gentle charm. My eyes narrowed. Tabitha never requested anything sweetly. Gunther gave a faint nod encouraging me to go.

"Fine," I crushed the sheets in my fist and headed toward the front door.

Once the heavy door closed behind us,

Tabitha turned and looked me steadily in the eyes. "Charlotte, you're acting different."

"Well, of course, I'm *different*," I told her flicking one hand in the air dismissing her observation. "I'm the head of a circus, I'm a super-powerful witch, I have other super-powerful witches after me, and your mother took my cat. How could you possibly think I would be the same?"

"See, that's what I mean," Tabitha said, pointing. "There. Right there."

"What?"

"That was one of the most arrogant boasts of bull I've ever heard come out of your mouth," Tabitha said, grinning despite the jolt her words conveyed. "I know about all the things that have happened to you, Charlotte. Heck, I knew about practically all of them before you ever showed back up here."

"So you knew your mother would steal my cat?"

"Wow," Tabitha drawled, the smile wavering. "What is this, a game of wits? See who can slap the most effective verbal blow on the other? Is *this* who you are now?"

"You don't know who I am now," I responded.

"No, Charlotte, *you* don't know who you are

now," Tabitha retorted, crossing her arms. "I've only been around you and your merry band of mythical creatures for a few days, and I already see things you don't even seem to have recognized."

"Oh, yeah, such as?"

"At the Makepeace Circus, Gunther no longer has his mother. Or his father. They both live with you. His new sister, here, with you," she replied, pain echoing through her words. "I've talked to him, tried to get to know him, and he's in *agony*, Charlotte," she added tenderly. She grabbed my hands and held them tight. "Everything that drives his life is here. Everything that makes his life worth living is here, with you."

"I...I don't see..."

"You don't see," Tabitha smiled, brushing the hair from my face with a soft touch. "The Charlotte I knew was sincere but kind. Skeptical, but loving. I know I lost it with you and Aidan pulling the wool over my eyes," she told me, inclining her head. "I was resentful, and I shouldn't have pushed you both away like I did. I know that you were trying to make me happy. You just went about it the wrong way."

"Thanks for saying that," I told her.

Her confession and apology touched me so

much I almost overlooked that she just said I was treating my boyfriend like dirt and being blind to his pain.

"But Charlotte, don't repeat my mistake," she warned. "I got so wrapped up in the lie I neglected everything else about our friendship. And then I lost it. You're so wrapped up in this Thirteenth Witch business you're neglecting the people around you. Well, not neglecting, really..."

I waited.

"Bob said that it was tough for you to let anyone help you in the beginning," she went on. Tabitha smirked. "I get that. I could even see it in my head. But Charlie? I gotta tell you, hon— you've gone to the opposite end of that. You are not the center of the universe, but you act like it. A lot. You're *losing* yourself in all this."

I should have been offended by what Tabitha was saying. I wasn't sure that I could trust her, and Fiona and Anya clearly had their suspicions about her.

Yet the whole conversation with her felt so familiar, so comfortable. I could sense that she meant well, and I knew that she could see the changes in me when no one else could. The witch in me didn't trust her completely, but the person I used to be?

Mickwac Charlotte knew that Tabitha would never do anything to hurt me.

"We're not Tabby and Charlie anymore," I sighed. My memories flipped through the two of us sunning ourselves on the college commons deck, attending a production of *Wicked* and arguing over which one of us was Elphaba and which one was Galinda. Tabitha consoling me when my umpteenth date went awry after I saw some fragment of nastiness in my date's head.

"We *are*, though," she insisted. "Our history remains with us. Your talent made you one of the most compassionate people I've ever found. Sure, you were hard sometimes. Yes, you were rigid sometimes. Even judgmental. But you always loved other people, and you were always there for them."

I sat down hard on the steps to the…drug house? Dropping my elbows on my knees, I cradled my head in my chin. "I didn't realize I was coming off as mean," I admitted after Tabitha sat beside me, silent, for a few minutes. "Especially not to Gunther."

"Oh, I'd say you're coming off *especially* mean to Gunther," Tabitha said.

I looked down.

"Look, I'm not saying this to beat you up

about it," my friend said. She brought her arm around me. "I get the sense that not many people can speak plainly to you now. Maybe they're all overwhelmed by your super-powered witch thing, but *I'm* not. To me, you're still just Charlie, my friend. And I get to point out when my friend is acting like a giant ass. Lovingly, of course," she smirked.

I half-smiled.

"You're only human," Tabitha said. I shifted my head.

"I'm not, though," I told her. "I'm a witch. For you, that's a spiritual path. For me, it's a species. It's a realm."

"It's a fraction of *my* realm," Tabitha disagreed. "This is the *mortal* world. We just let you live in it —I'm not suggesting that to be ugly, either," she said as my eyes blazed. "I'm truly not. That's not some kind of threat. But *I* know the history. There was a mortal-paranormal war. And *we* won. There are millions of us, and there are only thousands of you. You add color to the human world. We don't add color to *your* world. It's ours. Not yours."

I didn't know what to say to her. Her confidence in her human-ness, her delight and satisfaction in that was...strange to me. So many of the paranormals I knew were so full of themselves, so sure that the genuine authority of the world rested in their magic and not with the humans. They usually talked of mortals as nothing more than inconveniences or, at worst, threats.

Sarah Stevens's desperation to turn into one of us was a case in point. None of us *wished* to become human…

The image of the Magical Midway citizens, all donning a humanoid shape, burst across my mind. The ghosts clinging to their human countenances, shape-shifting paranormals using magic to present as human as they could.

Why a circus? Why something on display for mortals?

Maybe Tabitha was right. Maybe there was a lot I bought at face value because it was easier than working out what was underneath it all.

I got up, and we hugged. I resolved to get back in touch with who I had been when I took my place at the Magical Midway—

Until we heard a car door slam from the front of the house, and Raven Goodfellow's figure flashed through my mind.

"We have to hide!" I spat as we ran back inside the small bungalow.

CHAPTER 5

THE LANKY GOTH UNLOCKED THE DOOR TO THE cottage and stepped inside. Flipping the switch, he illuminated the room but didn't appear to see any of us tucked away in the shadows watching him. It could have been that we hid really well, but it was more likely that Raven was clueless to all the eyes on him.

"I'm bulletproof," he sung to himself as he smiled and tapped his hand against his thigh. "Empower me and watch me rise, get out of my way before I hypnotize," he singsonged. I didn't recognize it, but it wasn't surprising. I hadn't had a lot of time to listen to the radio of late. "There!"

Raven jumped and lunged toward the shelves that Gunther had been looking through just moments before. Climbing up on a chair, he grabbed a leather-bound book from the very top shelf and dropped down. "Stupid cat. More stubborn than she said it would be."

I leaned forward without thinking, and Tabitha grabbed me. *If you give away we're here, we can't follow him,* Tabitha thought so hard at me it echoed through my brain like a shout in an empty cavern. *I know this sucks, Charlotte, but you have to stay hidden. He's the best clue we have right now.*

I knew she was right, but it killed me to sit and do nothing.

Gunther walked out of the corner and stepped steadily toward Raven. I gasped, but he told us to stay still. "He can't see or hear me, I made sure of it," Gunther said softly. Pressing my hand over my mouth, I watched my boyfriend lean down and read the title of the book that Raven clutched in his sweaty palm. "*The Capture and Turning of Monsters,*" he read quietly. "The year on the book is 1872. It doesn't look that old, though."

Raven's phone buzzed, and he fished it out of his pocket, tapping the screen with his thumb. "I've got the book," he said. He placed the phone on the book and cradled both in his arms. "It was right where you said it was."

"Is my husband at the house? Maybe with his

crippled tart of a girlfriend?" Sarah Stevens asked Raven, her response echoing through the speaker. Tabitha tensed next to me as she recognized her mother's voice through the speaker-phone.

"I didn't check the main house. You told me to get the book, so I went into the bungalow, and I got the book," Raven replied haughtily.

"Well, check," Mrs. Stevens spat. "Now that we have the beings we need, everyone will be after us. At least Tabitha's at that circus keeping an eye on Charlotte." My stomach plummeted to my feet. Gunther turned to stare at Tabitha, his eyes narrowing. She froze, her face turning white. "We'll be able to find her when the time comes. I want to make sure we can find him, too."

"What about *my* mother?" Raven asked, heading toward the door.

"The high priestess? She's unimportant now," Sarah answered. Raven hesitated.

"But you said—"

"I changed my mind. If she had left with me, maybe things would have been different." The woman's voice cracked with anger through the phone. "Now that she's stuck at the circus with those monsters? Forget her, Raven. She's lost."

"She's my—"

"Bring me the book!" Sarah yelled, and the phone clicked.

Raven Goodfellow stood in the front hallway, his skinny shoulders tensing with fury. "It wasn't supposed to be like this," Raven said to himself, his voice barely above a whisper. "I didn't sign up for this. Sure, okay, my mother can be a pain, but...I didn't want anyone to get hurt..."

For a moment, for just a moment, I thought Raven Goodfellow was coming to his senses. For a moment, just a moment, I thought his conscience was getting the better of him, and he was moving out of his codependent fog and into clarity.

"Except for the beasts of the circus," he scoffed, shoving his phone back into his pocket. "Those accursed demons will suffer for all this."

With a delirious laugh, Raven walked out, slamming the door behind him.

"Explain," Kyle demanded as he stepped toward Tabitha. Bob's face contorted in confusion as he struggled between his duty to protect me and the affection he had built up for her. "What did your mother mean? You were keeping an eye on Charlotte?"

"Honestly, I don't know." Tabitha shook her head, her courage gone and her eyes nervous. "I swear, I wouldn't do anything to hurt Charlotte, Kyle."

"Aidan? Is she telling the truth? Can you see into her past?" Kyle asked his boyfriend. Aidan's eyes were glazed, unfocused, and he swayed on his feet. "Aidan?"

"He doesn't look good," Gunther said as he stepped forward.

"What's wrong with him?" Tabitha asked.

"Maybe we should ask *you* that," Kyle said and put his arm around the swaying past reader. The centaur and Gunther helped Aidan over to a chair. His face was even ashier than before.

"Could this place be warded somehow?" I asked Gunther. "Like the Magical Midway? Can humans do that?"

"He looked a little peaked back at the Midway, too." Fortuna stepped out from behind Kyle. Moving to face Aidan, she leaned over and peered deeply into his bloodshot eyes. The room was quiet except for Aidan's uneven, labored breathing.

"Something is inside of there with him." She

stood up after a few minutes and rubbed her forehead. "I'm sensing more than one energy, and that second presence doesn't want me poking around. It's…defensive."

"What do you mean *something*?" I asked her alarmed.

"I don't know," she said, turning to me. "It could be a second soul or a binding spell with an animated purpose? I've never come across it before."

"The Witches' Council again?" Gunther asked, shuddering as he remembered Mina World and her takeover of his body when his father was ill.

"I wish I could tell you," Fortuna said. "Like I said, whatever it is doesn't want me poking around in there. It's stronger than I am."

"Every step we take puts more of this mystery in the past," Gunther pointed out as he leaned over Aidan. "More comes into clarity. Aidan could help us more and more as he came into contact with people that had acted against us."

"So you think to keep us from getting that clarity, someone's put him out of commission? I could see that," Kyle said. "But how? Is he poisoned, is it magic? A spell? Is he in any danger?"

"I don't think so, but I can't see a lot," Fortuna
shook her head.

"Maybe Charlotte should try," Gunther said.

"Fortuna's actually a more powerful telepath
than I am," I told him. "If what she did isn't
revealing anything helpful, I doubt I'll pick up on
anything. I can try, though." I concentrated and
reached out to Aidan's mind, but all I picked up
was a gray haziness that obfuscated all of his
thoughts in a balmy mist.

"If something has weakened the past reader, I
suggest bringing him back to the protected
grounds at once," Bob insisted. Though he stood
beside Tabitha, there was a distance between
them now that hadn't been there before. "It is not
safe for a paranormal to be in the human world
in a weakened state."

"I agree," Tabitha said.

"No one asked you," Kyle said. The front door
opened, and we all froze.

"I also agree," Devana said as she stepped into
the room. I startled at the sudden appearance of
the huntress. She had been so quiet that I
honestly forgot she was there. Though since she
came in from outside, I guess she *wasn't* here.

"Where did you come from?" I asked her.

"I am a huntress," she shrugged casually. "I

sneaked out after the young man and followed him to the place he dropped off the book."

"I didn't even see you *leave*," Bob said in shock.

"As I said, I am a huntress," she smiled proudly. With a quiet nobility tinged by amusement, she winked at Bob. "If you could see me stalking my prey, I would not be much of a huntress, would I?"

She had a point.

"The place is a grotto, a large one, and it feels like a place of power," she told me. "I located Samson at the bottom of the grotto."

"The same place they held Tabitha?" Gunther asked with some confusion. "Why would they go back to a location they know we're aware of?"

"As I said, it is a place of power," Devana repeated. "There are not that many places in the human world that meet along the veins of the earth's blood."

"The earth's blood?"

"Water. It is the lifeblood of the earth, necessary for all living things," she answered serenely. "The grotto lies at a convergence of underground water, of ley lines, making it a place of power."

"A vortex," Gunther said.

"Yes, precisely," Devana nodded.

"Wait a minute, how did you get out to the grotto and back here so fast?" I asked Devana. "That place is nearly an hour away."

"I am a huntress," she said yet again as if that explained everything.

"Huntress witches have an ability none of the rest of us have," Gunther explained to me, still leaning over Aidan. "Well, several abilities we don't have. Probably more than we're aware of," Gunther said, half-smiling at Devana. "One ability I know about is the ability to explore a timeline of the hunt."

"Explore a timeline. What does that mean?"

"Once Raven Goodfellow got in his car and started his journey to bring Sarah Stevens the book she requested, I could follow the conclusion of that choice to see where it would lead. I did so faster than he was able to complete the journey."

"In your mind, you mean?"

Devana shook her head no.

"So, wait—you got there before *he* got there?" I stared at her.

Devana nodded with pride.

"And *back here* before he even arrived *there*?" I asked incredulously.

The huntress nodded once again.

"They are feared because they always seem a step ahead of their prey," Gunther said.

"We seem so because we *are* so," Devana said.

I stared at Devana. "Are there any caveats to this power?"

"One."

"And that is?"

"The prey must be alive."

Fortuna and Gunther left with Aidan to return him to the Magical Midway via the Makepeace Circus. Gunther didn't want to leave me. "It's not safe out here right now," he told me, his eyes glancing over to Tabitha. I assured him that with Devana, Bob, and Kyle around me I was unlikely to be surprised by a sneak attack.

"It won't take you long," I told him. He looked unconvinced, but he couldn't argue when I reminded him I was the only one that could talk to Samson telepathically. He had to be the one to send Aidan back to the circus grounds, and he had to be closer to the location we sent them from to do it. "If I went back there, it would take too much time. After we figure out what's going on with Tabitha, we'll head to the grotto."

Reluctantly, Gunther left with a groggy, out of it Aidan.

"Let's talk," I said to the remaining group as the front door closed, cursing myself for not getting Fortuna to dig around in Tabitha's mind before she left. I didn't have confidence in my ability to read my friend.

I didn't want to believe that Anya and Fiona were right about her.

"I don't know," Tabitha said as we sat down before any of us had even asked her a question. "I don't know what my mother meant. I promise you I had no part in whatever this power theft thing is that she thinks she's doing. You *know* me, Charlotte," Tabitha pleaded with me. "We've been friends since the beginning of freshman year. I never, ever *lied* to *you*. I will not start now."

Ouch. That hurt, a little zinged barb to remind me that on dishonesty road, Tabitha had several miles to run before catching up with me.

Even so. I lied to Tabitha about a fake boyfriend. She might be lying to me about a conspiracy to take the circus from me and give it to her power-crazed mother.

"If this were just some run of the mill distortion of the truth, Tabitha, it wouldn't bother me that much," I told her. "People are dishonest sometimes. I get that. Hell, I have to be dishonest about who I am when I walk out in the world. I get it."

"That's not what this is," Kyle argued with me.

"I know that," I told him. "This is a conspiracy, and what her mother said implied she was part of it. I get it."

"I sense no malice from the human, boss," Bob said.

"You sensed no malice from her mother, either, lares—and her mother walked out with the guardian," Kyle told the Roman. "Can you even sense deception?"

Bob looked like he wanted to argue but then shook his head no. "Only malice," he answered quietly. "And if it's deliberately hidden, sometimes not then."

"Is this some lares power I don't know about?"

"No, boss," Bob shook his head no. "I just know people."

"You don't know me," Tabitha told him, pointing a finger. Turning to me, she grabbed my hand. "But you do, Charlotte. Trust me. I would never do anything to hurt you."

"If you don't think this would hurt her? That statement still wouldn't be a denial," Kyle pointed out, and she glared at him angrily.

"I swear on my life that I am not playing an active part in my mother's conspiracy in any way, shape, or form." Tabitha raised her hand and placed the other one over her heart. "If this is a lie, may the gods strike me dead where I stand."

"You're sitting," Bob said as he shifted next to her.

"Oh, Bob," I sighed and covered my face in my hands.

CHAPTER 6

As we left the bungalow and walked toward the car, Darius Stevens barreled around the corner of the main house. His face was splotchy and red with dark eyes that flashed fury. Everyone paused, suspended in mid-step as Mr. Stevens stomped straight for us.

"What are you people doing on my property?" he demanded. With an abrupt lurch, he halted and squinted at the appearance of his daughter. I realized with a start that Tabitha and her father had not seen each other since before her entombment beneath the cavern. "Tabitha? Is that you?"

Wow. Was he actually *teary-eyed*? Seriously? The anger that had infused Mr. Stevens's words faded and his question sounded almost tender. There was a softness I *hadn't* expected from the man. Not based on my own interactions with him, or Tabitha's stories about him, or Sarah's description of him, or Samantha Goodfellow's account of him.

"Hey, Dad," Tabitha answered. She held up a hand to us as she stepped toward her father. The dark shadows of the patio seemed to envelop the two of them in the corner as he pressed her tightly into his arms. "What are you doing here?"

"Looking for you," he said. "Your mother—"

"I know, Dad," she cut him off as they embraced. My eyes narrowed. "I realize it was Mom and Raven that had me kidnapped."

"Wait a minute, wait a minute, wait a minute. Just wait," I crossed my arms and stared, trying to make sense of the scene unfolding before me. "When Aidan and I showed up to talk to you, you sounded as if you couldn't care less whether Tabitha lived or died."

"Do I know you?" Darius asked, his arm still around Tabitha.

"You don't remember me?" I challenged him. "Aidan and I came to your house to talk to your wife about Tabitha's disappearance. You arrived while we were—"

"I *recall* you and Aidan coming to talk to my wife and me," Darius told me coldly and tilted his head. "My point is whether I *knew* you. And I did not. I didn't know you then, and I had no reason to *trust* you. Not then, and not now. For all I knew, *you* had snatched my daughter."

Well.

I looked carefully at Darius Stevens, his arm folded around Tabitha as if she was a precious possession he had just retrieved. The coldness I perceived in him had been replaced by…not *warmth*, but a *protectiveness*. A protectiveness wrapped in a wary suspicion.

"Dad, be nice to Charlotte. Without her I'd still be stuck in that cave." I caught that Tabitha did not disclose what cave she had been stuck in, and her father didn't ask any questions. "What do you know about what's going on here, Dad? And tell me the truth," Tabitha asked, tugging away from her father. "Not the usual line of garbage you tell me about what you do for a living."

"Maybe we should go inside," Tabitha's father responded, His eyes darted toward the towering brick walls that enclosed the backyard. "I'm sure your mother had more than Raven spying for her."

"Look, not to be too much of a pain, but right

now, I'm not trusting a single person involved in any of this," I told him, stepping back. "Your wife and your daughter have both warned me you are, essentially, a techno-gangster living on the edge of the law seeking to supplant Michael Hayden as the town criminal kingpin."

"Your point?" Darius asked without refuting it.

What *was* it with the criminals in this town? They were all so blasé about their actions. A corrupt police department must breed an awful lot of complacency in its felonious citizens.

"My point is *I* don't know *you*," I told him. Devana and Kyle moved closer, the two of them flanking me as if we were arranging for battle. Bob stood apart from everyone, his face a writhing mess of emotions as he tried to puzzle out the best thing to do.

"That's a fair statement," Darius nodded. "But no one knows my wife better than I do, and I am sure that you don't have the entire picture of what's going on, despite your superpowers."

Was there anyone left in this town that didn't know I was a witch?

"Your wife wants magic. My magic—"

"I'm going to ask you *again* to go inside," Darius's voice thundered as he peered around the darkness again. "Too many people know about you and realize what you are as it is. Having this discussion here can only result in even more risk to us all. If you continue having this conversation out in the open like this? You'll be having it with yourself."

Darius Stevens cleared his throat loudly and strode with deliberate steps toward the front of the house.

Bob, Kyle, Devana and I glanced into each other's faces to find mirrored expressions of mistrust and uneasiness.

"Guys, my dad just wants to talk, I'm sure," Tabitha said. She smiled at me with a sincerity I was no longer sure I could trust. "Come on, let's go."

My heart raced as I followed Tabitha and contemplated whether I could rely on what I perceived coming from my old friend, or whether I was letting my feelings lead me down a path that would lose me my powers, my circus, and kill my cat in the process.

"Oh my gosh, you guys, hi!" Melissa Hayden said with surprise. Her eyes scanned over us. As they fell upon her witchcraft study companion, her eyes widened in amazement. "Tabitha! Oh my gosh, you're okay! Oh my gosh!" Melissa jumped up and dashed to envelop her confused friend in a hug. With a clumsy flop, she toppled into Tabitha's arms. "Why didn't you tell me, Darius?"

Darius? She calls Tabitha's father by his first name?

"I wasn't aware that Tabitha had been rescued, Melissa," Darius responded. He strode over to the couch, grabbed Melissa's cane, and walked it over to her. With a brief smile, he continued. "If I had known, I would have let you know."

"Oh, it doesn't matter, I'm just so glad that you're okay! I always knew you were okay, though. But I'm so pleased that I was right!" she smiled broadly as she slipped her arm into the crutch and grabbed the handle. "Did you see how far I went without the cane, Darius? Did you?" the young woman asked breathlessly.

"I did," Tabitha's father acknowledged.

What on earth was going on here?

"What brings you here, Melissa?" Kyle asked respectfully. Bob and Devana watched the scene unfolding with confusion. Bob didn't know who Melissa Hayden was, and Devana was only vaguely acquainted with the gangster's younger sister. "We're surprised to find you here."

"Darius is trying to figure out why my legs work now, aren't you, Dar?" the girl said as she cast a sideways glance at the older man. Her cheeks glowed as she beamed at him.

Dar?

"Yes, that's right," he coughed, shifting away from her blushing schoolgirl expression to pour himself a drink. "Just a personal side project, that's all."

The rush of attraction that flowed out from Melissa when she looked at Darius Stevens left me sure that the college student's interest in the older man was about more than his intelligence. I looked sharply at Tabitha, trying to get a read on whether she was aware; I picked up nothing from her.

If her friend and outer-court coven mate from Avalon Grove having a crush on her father bothered her, there was nothing inward or outward that confirmed it.

I speculated whether this crush was a one way or two-way street. Was Darius Stevens having an affair with the college-age friend of his daughter? I shuddered in disgust.

Then my blood ran cold as I recalled a conversation.

Melissa had come to my parents' house to let me know that she thought Tabitha was probably fine. Why? Because she had seen Mr. Stevens at a burger joint and he dismissed her concern. I asked her how often she had seen Tabitha and her father.

"Oh, I don't know, maybe two or three times? Rarely, really. I was super surprised that he recognized me enough to say hi. I didn't think he even knew who I was."

"I thought you had hardly ever met Mr. Stevens?" I asked Melissa.

"I…what? No, I never said that," Melissa responded with a blush.

"You did."

"I didn't," Melissa responded again more emphatically, blushing even redder as her eyes skipped toward Darius, and then Tabitha. "You must be misremembering."

I considered her silently, my skeptical mind working overtime as I struggled to put the pieces together.

Then I realized I didn't care.

I just needed my cat. Once I got Samson, none of this would matter anymore. They could all have whatever affairs they wanted, hack into whatever they wanted, engage in a mob war if they wanted. It had nothing to do with me, my circus, or the paranormal world.

"Look, I just want my cat back. That's it," I said as I swallowed a lump in my throat. "If the information about your wife will help me do that, let's get to it. If not, I have to go."

Devana shifted to my right. The energy surrounding her resembled that of a coiled snake ready to strike. How she could be so dignified and subdued and yet so predatory in the space of the same moment baffled me.

"I don't talk in front of cops," Darius said as he waved at Kyle.

"Kyle is no longer with the police department," Tabitha told him. "He works for Charlotte's circus now."

"Doing what?"

"Head of Security." Bob raised his eyebrow.

"And who are these people?" Darius asked, pointing at Bob and Devana.

"Dude, just *talk!*" I demanded, pointing my finger at Darius. The lawgiver ring (which imbued me with the power to compel guilty paranormals to confess, freeze accused paranormal criminals, and coerce witnesses to spill their guts) glowed for a brief moment.

Darius Stevens's eyes glassed over as he sat down upon a velvet-covered wing chair, crossed his legs, and calmly spilled his guts.

"My wife and I despise one another," Darius said, pausing to sip his bourbon. I stared, startled, at my finger, shaking my hand as if the ring was bugged. "I'm sure Tabitha could reveal to you how long we have disliked one another and how profoundly we disdain this marriage. Can't you, dear?"

"I...I...what the heck did you do to my father, Charlotte?" Tabitha breathed out as she gawked. "Okay, sure, I knew that about my parents, but we don't just *say* it out in the *open* like that."

"What's wrong?" Melissa demanded.

"I'm a lawgiver," I told her, glowering, and shaking my hand. "This ring lets me make paranormals talk if they've committed some crime. Mr. Stevens, *are* you a paranormal?"

"What's a paranormal?" he asked bewildered.

"What's a lawgiver?" Melissa asked Tabitha. Tabitha held up her palm to silence the young woman. Watching her father closely, her face was unreadable. I went on questioning him.

"Are you a witch, centaur, were-animal of any kind?"

"They initiated me into Avalon Grove in college, so I am technically a witch," he explained. "I haven't practiced in years, though."

"Not *that* kind of witch," I murmured, dismissing the mythic-based cosplay that was human witchcraft. Devana's face was drawn and pale as she stood next to Bob. The lares guard looked gobsmacked.

"Could he be one and not *know*?" Tabitha asked.

"Anybody could be, I guess," I shrugged. "Has he ever been to the Magical Midway? It's set up shop here almost every year."

"He took me when I was about ten."

"Then no," I shook my head. "Whatever latent paranormal genetics he had would have awakened when he came onto the grounds. He *shouldn't* be subject to the lawgiver ring. It *shouldn't* be affecting him like this."

Samson would know what was going on here.

Devana stepped closer to Darius, his eyes still glazed. He peered up at her and smiled dreamily while she narrowed her eyes and scrutinized his face keenly. "You are an *exquisite* woman. So stern and severe. Perhaps *you* should question me. Or give me an order," his eyes drooped as he reached a hand to hers, his voice filled with the *most* inappropriate yearning.

"Oh, my gosh, Dad, you're *revolting*," Tabitha popped up beside him and whacked his hand away from the huntress witch. The man turned toward his daughter and laughed. She rolled her eyes.

"He is not a paranormal. At least, he is not one of us," Devana said. She twisted his head back forcefully to face her and scanned the man's soft eyes. "There is something within him, however, something I could track if I needed to. Even though he is mortal, there is a spark of what we are. Just a spark, no more than that. But it is enough."

"Enough to what?" Tabitha asked.

"What are you people talking about?" Melissa asked. Raising a brow, the perky young lady leaned back. "Dar, what are they all talking about?"

"Mel, be quiet," Tabitha shushed her friend.

"It is in *her* as well," Devana turned to Melissa in astonishment and moved toward her. "And more than the other one. Much more." Devana jerked her thumb toward Darius.

"*What's* in me? What are you talking about?" she demanded, backing away from Devana's advance. The huntress witch searched the girl's gaze even as Melissa held her palms up to block Devana from studying her.

"She *is* mortal," Devana pronounced.

"Of course I'm mortal!" Melissa responded heatedly. "Will someone tell me what on earth you're all talking about?"

"And me?" Tabitha asked, her quiet question heavy with dread. Devana stared at her for a brief moment and then gave a swift nod. Concern flickered Tabitha's eyes, and she swallowed. Turning to me, Tabitha whispered a question I didn't have the answer to.

"What is going on here?"

CHAPTER 7

DARIUS STEVENS STARTED TALKING, AND HE DIDN'T cease until he had unpacked everything he knew about his wife's plot to take over the world. Whatever that little spark was that subjected him to my magic finger of unburdening, that spark set his mouth on fire.

Besides describing what we previously learned, Darius confessed to having embezzled millions of dollars from a former governor, dodging taxes by parking his money in an offshore haven, having affair after affair for what *sounded* like Tabitha's entire life (including three at that very moment).

It was in a vindictive rage that Sarah Stevens devised a plot to end her husband's womanizing ways forever. That she would be hugely influential, have extraordinary powers, and infinite money was just a bonus.

Even Kyle, the former police detective, couldn't hide his shock.

"So, you're saying that your wife is trying to steal my circus so she can blast a hole in your head with my power because you cheated on her again and again with younger women? Wouldn't just whacking you in the head with a shovel accomplish this a lot faster?" I asked him. "This is a complicated plot just to punish you for being a jerk."

"However many people know about magic and witchcraft, the police probably won't," Tabitha told me as she glared at her father. "If Dad got slammed in the head with a shovel, you can be certain that the police would look to Mom first."

"Even though he's some kind of techno-gangster dude?"

"She would take over everything," Kyle pointed out. "We would always look at whoever has the most to gain."

"I thought you weren't a police officer anymore?" Darius asked calmly. "You seem to use 'we' with a natural comfort, son."

"I'm not, but it's not like I left all my training back in my human life. And do not, under any circumstances, call me son."

"You *seem* human," Darius asked, his eyes large.

"I just heard the story of how bad you screwed over your family," Kyle snorted and crossed his arms. "I'm not sure you're a great judge of anybody's humanity, so you just mind your own business over there, Casanova."

"Darius Stevens, you are the lowest human being I've ever met my life," Melissa Hayden hissed as she smashed his shinbone with her crutch. "Are you telling me the whole time you and I have been dating you've been seeing two other women? Besides your wife?"

"They mean nothing to me, dear. I love *you*," Darius said. Tabitha made a retching noise.

"I thought he couldn't lie when he was under the lawgiver power?" Kyle asked me.

"He can't lie to *me*. I have no idea whether he can lie to anyone else. Hey, Darius, do you love Melissa Hayden?"

"Of course not," he swung to me. "I'm only connected to the child to get intelligence on her brother. If I can figure out how she's walking when she shouldn't be? That will just be an economic bonus." Melissa's face turned several shades of crimson as *his* look turned lecherous. "And the side benefits of this plot aren't bad, either."

"Dad!" Tabitha shouted. "You just don't know when to shut up, do you? You are so revolting. I cannot believe you're my father."

"I can't believe that *you* were actually using *me!*" Melissa exclaimed indignantly.

"Why would you think you could count on him?" Kyle asked, trying not to smirk. "He's twice your age and married. He's a felon. On what planet do *you* live that you determined he was someone to be trusted?"

Melissa scowled at Kyle, but she didn't answer.

As Tabitha, Melissa and her father considered, noisily, all that he had shared with them, I nodded to Bob to keep an eye on the three. Motioning to Devana and Kyle, we stepped away from the incensed group.

"I feel like we're getting away from the top priority, here, which is Samson," I said to both of them. "I don't care about Darius's affairs, or money, or Sarah's revenge. I just want my cat. None of this has anything to do with me. Let's just leave them here and go to the cavern."

"What about Jeannie?" Devana asked softly. I spun to look at her, her fierce gaze startling me. "I don't mean to suggest that you do not care about your uncle's girlfriend, or that you are unconcerned by her death. But the death of an immortal took place on the circus grounds amid this—"

"Drama? Western telenovela? Texas two-steppin' histrionic display of avarice, corruption, and treachery?" I suggested helpfully.

Kyle chuckled, but his expression looked troubled.

"Jeannie, an immortal, is dead. Aidan has been taken ill," Devana said and Kyle grimaced. "In one day, two resources that we had—two essential resources—have been removed from the field."

"And we can deal with those matters *after* we get Samson," I told her. I peeked at Tabitha sitting serenely, observing us. "There are two separate issues going on here, and the biggest priority is Samson. *He's* the one in peril. All of us are, too, every minute he remains with them."

"Maybe not," Kyle looked at Melissa and Darius on the couch. "*He's* a resource, too. If you put all of *this* aside," Kyle said and waved in the direction of the still arguing couple, "in the past twenty-four hours, we've seen *three* principal players taken out. Samson, then Jeannie, then Aidan. That *can't* be a fluke."

"And *we* do not yet realize why young Aidan has taken ill," Devana added.

"Even paranormals have to just get the flu sometimes, right?" I asked them confidently. "Maybe it's only that." Both Kyle and Devana stared at me expressionless, their silence saying more about my illogical straw-grasp than their words could have.

Tabitha's kidnapping had seemed too easy, too mundane (if you could call a coven of witches trapping someone in a submerged cave mundane). We had dismissed the possibility that the Witches' Council was involved in any of this. Everything had looked straightforward.

Raven admitted to trapping Tabitha. He indicated that he was working for someone. Once Samson was stolen, that someone was clearly Sarah Stevens. Simple. Easy.

Wasn't it?

That Darius Stevens was a criminal, having a liaison with the sister of another criminal, that Michael Hayden (the older brother gangster) knew I was a witch, that Melissa Hayden was coven mates with Tabitha and Raven…

I groaned. "Yeah, okay. Maybe. What a mess this is. It's like a Gordian knot."

"As you get closer to the time of choosing, Ringmaster, the Council will no doubt step up their attempts to exclude you from the field as well," Devana said. "Ms. Elkins would have been wise to advise you of that."

"Oh, right, right," I said distractedly. "The Thirteenth Witch thing."

Devana snorted back a chuckle, and I stared at her in shock. I couldn't recall *ever* encountering the huntress witch's laugh before. Like, ever. Smile, sure. Laugh? Never. I looked at her and lifted my eyebrow.

"I just thought of what Ms. Elkins would say to you if she heard you shrug off being the Thirteenth Witch with such indifference." Devana cleared her throat and steadied her expression.

"Maybe she *shouldn't* be apathetic," Kyle said. He leaned forward and dropped his voice. "The missing people. The paranormal spark in these humans. What if Samson *isn't* the ultimate target of this little endeavor? What if the *whole thing* is a Witches' Council trap?"

"An ambush?" Devana leaned closer to Kyle.

"That would mean Tabitha's seizure was nothing more than a trial run, a demonstration of concept," I whispered, trying to keep my eyes from searching out my human friend. I failed, and our gazes met. I looked away hastily.

"And that someone likely works personally with the Witches' Council," Devana said.

The three of us turned and looked at the humans on the other side of the room. As I wondered if any of them was working with the Witches' Council to destroy our home, my eyes met Tabitha's again.

She peered back, silent.

CHAPTER 8

WE ALL LOADED INTO MY PARENTS' ENORMOUS SUV. The truck was so obscenely large it could precipitate an environmental protest all on its own, if it wasn't a magically powered hybrid. For the first time, I was thankful for the big boat.

"Watch them," I told Bob. He clambered in after the still angry Melissa and waited while she slid next to the still blissfully honest Darius. "You, too," I whispered to Devana, so Bob couldn't hear. Not that I couldn't count on him. It was that I didn't trust Melissa, Darius...

Okay, or Tabitha.

Pulling away from the Stevenses' house, I paused at the end of the street. A right turn would take us toward the grotto. A left one would take us back into town and toward my parents' house. My finger tapped against the steering wheel impatiently as I scanned back and forth.

Right or left.

Samson or help.

"Maybe it would be better to have your boyfriend with you," Tabitha said softly from the passenger side. "Just in case it is a trap." I turned to study at her, my empathic sense searching for a clue regarding her motivation. I saw forms in her head, flashes, and apprehension, but just as I tried to seize them mentally and inspect them, they popped like bubbles hitting the pavement.

"Are you informing me of that because you're *really* concerned about me or because you require both of us in the same place?" I asked, flinging the truck into park.

"I don't follow what you mean," Tabitha's eyes clouded.

"Forget it," I said. I twisted back and caught the gear stick just seconds after I let it go and turned the SUV left. "If you have anything to do with this, it's not like you would bother to tell me, anyway."

"I would. I don't. The grotto's the other way," Tabitha pointed out.

"Avalon Grove is this way," I told her as I headed for Samantha Goodfellow's pagan shop.

"Avalon Grove," Tabitha said, alarmed. "Why on earth are you going there?" I didn't respond.

"Do we think Samantha Goodfellow might have…the spark?" Devana asked from the backseat. I peered into the rear-view mirror at her and shrugged.

"I don't know, but she might have an explanation for it. We now know that her son is personally involved in whatever Sarah Stevens is doing. Maybe she has more insight now that she realizes her son's more of a bad seed than she thought."

"That poor woman," Tabitha murmured.

"Maybe," I said as we shot toward the plaza.

Soft lights twinkled through the front window of the arcane looking storefront. As we parked and disembarked, chimes and flutes echoed faintly in the darkness. Few cars were here this late at night, and most shops had long since closed.

"Bring him," I pointed to Darius. The older man was drunkenly smiling, his gaze wandering down to the posteriors of every woman who had the misfortune to walk in front of him. Tabitha wisely stayed out of her father's line of sight. Bob gripped the man tightly on his arm and gave a solemn nod.

The bell from the front door clanged as I yanked it open.

"Oh, Goddess, please protect my idiot son from his foolish thoughts and his even more stupid actions," Samantha Goodfellow's voice bellowed from the back room. "Let us wrap a protective light of white around him like a straightjack— um, a loving, white blanket! In the Goddess's name, so mote it be!"

"So mote it be," a soft harmony of women's voices answered her. Many hands clapped together.

"Whoah," Devana gasped and halted.

"What is it?" Kyle leaned over and set a hand on her shoulder, searching Devana's wide-eyed face.

"I *felt* that," she explained. She glanced at me and raised her eyebrow. "You didn't notice that? Like a vibration of…like the *spark*."

"It's the coven," Melissa said, pressing her way forward. "They're doing a protection ritual for Raven, it sounds like."

Samson, can you hear me? Damn it, cat, why can't

you answer? What good is this stupid telepathic link if it fails when everyone's life seems to be on the line?

I'm headed back, Gunther said. *Ms. Elkins is taking care of Aidan.*

Ms. Elkins? Are you sure his life isn't in danger?

Fortuna is remaining here with them.

Are you driving, or—

With a burst of light, Gunther appeared on his knees in the center of the magical shop. "Nope, no need for a car," he panted as he looked up and smiled. "What are we doing here?"

"Samantha Goodfellow—"

"Has a gun pointed right at your head, so you better just hold tight until I call the police unless you want a hole blown clean through ya!" The high priestess's shape appeared in the doorway accented by the distinct outline of a shotgun.

"Priestess, it's just us," Tabitha called out. "Melissa's with me, so's my dad. Charlotte's here with her friends, too."

"Goodness, child, don't scare me like that!" She lowered the weapon and used it as a cane to limp toward us. "Lock the front door. All we need is the townspeople to pick today to burn us all at the stake!"

Three young women, crouched over, wandered in from the hallway and into the dim glow of the main storefront as Gunther left to lock the door. Their eyes were wide, hands shaking, as they gawked at me.

"It is her?" one murmured.

"It must be, look at her aura!" another claimed.

"The goddess's handmaiden right here in Mickwac!" announced the third as she hurled herself down toward my feet. Once there, she kissed my dusty shoes.

"I, uh...I...What the hell is going on here?" I looked at Ms. Goodfellow. "Why is this girl caressing my sneakers?"

The girl peered up at me with crestfallen bewilderment. "You are the Goddess's most favored woman! I am worshiping you!"

"You're getting your face coated with dirt, is what you're doing," I told her. I leaned down and caught her gently by the arm to drag her up. "I work at a circus and have been staying at an animal shelter, no telling what else might be on those shoes."

The girl swooned as she came face to face with me.

"Door's bolted," Gunther said as he came back and settled beside me.

The three girls shrieked and threw themselves

down at my boyfriend's feet. Gunther stared at them in horror.

"Let me guess, the most favored man?" I asked the high priestess. She bowed. Devana stared at the writhing women as they delivered kiss after kiss to Gunther's ankles and wailed in rapture. "They sound a little more passionate about the most favored man than they do the goddess's handmaiden."

"You don't know much about what male gods represent in their adaptation of witchcraft, do you?" Tabitha smirked.

"Virility," Melissa said, grinning at me.

"Okay, time to get up," I sprang into action and removed each one from my boyfriend's exposed ankles and put them back on their feet. Their faces fell in anguish as I dragged them away a little less gently than before. "The goddess's handmaiden would like to demand that the humans lay off the most favored man, please. And thank you."

"*Anything* for you, Chosen One," the blonde woman beamed at me, but her eyes cut sideways toward a blushing Gunther. "And for you, Chosen One," she murmured with a wink.

"Chosen 'one' signifies that there's just one,

no?" I asked no one specific. Samantha nodded. "So how can we both be a chosen one?"

"Not all things are just one or the other," the priestess said. "In fact, true choices are often shades of gray upon layers of competing aspirations."

"Well put," Devana nodded and smiled. Because of course she agreed with the senseless, cryptic statement.

As the humans noticed Devana for the first time, their faces went white. The girl in front, a slender girl with dark hair and dark eyes, gave a formal curtsy. The brunettes behind her followed. Devana formally bowed back. Color did not return to their faces.

"High Priestess, may we welcome them to the circle?" the raven-haired one asked still warily looking at Devana. The other two nodded, and the three reminded me for a short moment of the World sisters with Mina at the helm. "It would be such a tremendous honor."

"And *I* haven't been back for a long time," Darius said from behind Tabitha. Samantha Goodfellow looked up sharply as his amused gaze met her astounded one. They stared at one another silently.

"Yes, let's move to the back room," Samantha

Goodfellow nodded. "We have plenty to talk about."

They had transformed the storage room into an elaborately decorated arcane ritual space. Ancient tapestries hung from the walls, a circle was drawn on the floor, and four pillar candles burned bright at a corresponding distance from one another at the configuration's edge.

"Wow," I murmured. "This looks nothing like before."

"We have become accomplished at quickly transforming our space for our purpose," Samantha said as she gestured to the mats within the circle.

"Ms. Goodfellow, are you feeling all right? After the drugs, I was a little worried," Kyle said. He reached out and helped the hefty woman to the one and only chair set up near what looked like a shrine.

"Yes, thank you, Kyle," she nodded as she sank down. Patting his arm, she smiled. "The effects dissipated rapidly after you found the patch and got rid of it."

"Look, we're sorry to cut short your ritual," I

said. "But you were the person who told us about Sarah, Darius, and Tabitha. You never pointed out that he had a thing with Melissa Hayden, never brought up that your son was deeply involved with Sarah Stevens. Now that it's clear Raven is in the thick of this thing, I sense you may be more involved than you let on."

The three human witches quietly got up, collected their mats, and planted them in a semi-circle around the foot of Samantha Goodfellow as I talked. They turned and faced me, expressions still awed but now just a shade wary.

Gunther and Devana quietly moved beside me to oppose them.

Tabitha, Kyle, and Bob stayed where they were, a muttering Darius and Melissa still arguing in whispers behind them.

"I may be more involved than I shared with you, Charlotte. But if I was, I was unaware of it at the time," she said, her smile strained.

"Were you drugged?" Gunther asked. She shook her head no.

"I was stupid," the high priestess said grimly as the humans protested. Samantha raised a ringed hand and palmed out with a melodramatic twist to stifle them. "Well, and at times someone drugged me, I'm sure. But I suspect that this came about because I was stupid."

"Explain," Kyle said gently.

"High Priestess—" the raven-haired girl objected.

"No, child," Samantha smiled at her, patting her hair. "It is time that my mistakes come into the light. Who better to condemn or absolve me than the chosen ones, the most favored of the Goddess? If I cannot expose my spirit to them, who are we?"

"But High Priestess—" another girl said, staring at Darius.

"Enough," Samantha Goodfellow cut off the protestations with a beleaguered weariness. "It is time that we all pay our prices, whatever they may be."

CHAPTER 9

"IT IS A PAINFUL THING, BEING UNABLE TO DECLARE who or what you are, what you've done," Samantha began as she glanced away from us and gazed at a spot on the wall. Tabitha turned and looked but, seeing nothing, shrugged and turned back to the older woman. "I am not suggesting that what we go through is anything like what you do," she smiled at me. "Just that humans have mysteries, too."

The three young women sitting at the high priestess's feet looked distressed. I still hadn't been formally introduced to them and had no idea of their names. They reminded me of a chorus from classical Greek dramas; in attendance not because they were personalities in their own right, but to reflect and color Samantha Goodfellow's story. The incense hovered around the room, giving the entire scene a surreal nature.

"It is said that when a witch does not want her acts seen, she should perform those activities during the dark of the moon," Samantha whispered. "It was during the dark of the moon I fell in love with Darius Stevens."

"Before he met my mother?" Tabitha asked.

The expression on Samantha's guilty face answered for her.

"This is all ancient history," Darius said hotly as he struggled to shove himself off the wall.

Melissa's eyes grew tight. She stared back and forth between the rotund priestess and the truth-drunk older man.

"No need to bring up all this garbage from the past," Tabitha's father added. He gave up and leaned back against the wall. Sliding down next to Melissa, he grabbed her hand, but she yanked it away with a glare.

"If only that were true," Samantha Goodfellow shot back. Her face flashed to fierce anger. "The darkness always gives way to the light. Things hidden rarely remain so. You would have known that if you ever paid mind to anything other than your *own* power. Your own needs."

Darius waved his hand dismissively while Tabitha's eyes locked on me, frozen. Her emotions were a chaotic swirl of dread and apprehension as if she balanced on the edge of a precipice. "Do you realize what she's about to say?" I asked her. Tabitha shook her head no.

"Tabitha is an innocent in all this, Charlotte, as is my poor son," the high priestess insisted. The Greek chorus of college students turned to Tabitha and smiled. Her voice reverberated with sincerity, though whether it was because it was true or she considered it to be true, I couldn't tell.

"I don't know that Charlotte believes any of us, High Priestess," Tabitha said, still looking at me.

"I'm having a hard time trusting *myself* at the moment," I answered. Gunther reached out and pressed my hand. The consistent pressure of his strength made me feel somewhat more settled than before, but not by much. "I came back to find my lost friend and assumed that would be the end of it. Instead, I find myself entangled in a...I don't even know what this is."

"No, I see you do not," Samantha said,

exhaling as tears began a slow drip from her eyes. "And I *am* sorry that my mistake has led unquestionably to the peril of those you care about."

"What mistake? Falling in love with that imbecile?" I asked, pointing at Darius.

"No," she swung her head. "Acting on that love in betrayal of my coven mate and friend, Sarah—"

Samantha's words roused Darius from his dreamy lawgiver-induced haze, and his tone became fierce as he sought to thrust himself up again. If he knew what she was planning on saying, it appeared to be the first moment he truly believed she would say it. "Woman, you need to stop—" he started, but Bob's solid grip slammed him back to the floor and halted his words. Darius shot a menacing look at the lares but remained where Bob held him.

"And bearing the product of my dishonor," Samantha finished.

There was a moment of utter silence.

"Oh, no," Tabitha whispered, struggling to her knees. Her eyes widened, and it was the first time I had seen Tabitha truly rattled. "Please don't say what I think you're about to say. No, no, no, no, you can't mean that…"

"Yes," Samantha whispered back, her sad eyes

filled with tears. "Raven is your brother, and the secret, illegitimate son of Darius Stevens. And we never told either of you."

Samantha Goodfellow paused, closing her eyes as if the lack of sight could blot out the truth of what she confessed. When she opened them, her eyes met Tabitha's.

"Or your mother."

The room erupted into shrieks of recrimination.

Darius bellowed at the stricken high priestess. Her head bent, she took her former lover's heaps of fury, repudiation, and insult without taking her eyes from Tabitha. Tabitha stared in confusion at her father as if she had never seen him before.

There was no reaction from Melissa.

"Your lies," Tabitha hissed. She rose up, tears streaking down her bright red cheeks as she stared down at her father. "It's *always* your lies, or your selfishness, or your hubris—"

"I'm your *father*," Darius snapped at her from his place on the floor. "Watch how you talk to me."

"My *father*? And how many *other* people's

father are you?" she challenged him. "We didn't leave the coven because of your contempt for witchcraft," Tabitha said accusingly, her eyes shining with fury. "We left our entire life when I was a kid because Raven and I were close! Admit it!"

"What do you mean?" I asked her.

"Raven and I were close to the same age," she spun toward me, her hands squeezed into fists as she turned her back on Darius. "We were young and played together growing up. Right before we left the group, Raven started joking that he would marry me. I mean, we were young, it was *innocent*, but it must have freaked the two of them out," she turned and glared daggers at her father. "Because he *knew*! He knew, and he couldn't say!"

"I knew nothing!" he thundered, his hands balled into fists so tight his knuckles were white. The angry man pushed against the wall and slid up to a standing position. "We left because I didn't want—"

"You're a *liar*!" she pivoted to face him. "Whatever Mom is, Dad? *You made her that way!*" Rage poured out from Tabitha, icy rage covered in a fire of resentment. Bob stepped in front of Darius, blocking him against the wall with his shoulder to protect Darius from Tabitha's advance. She reached out to strike the lares.

Samantha Goodfellow sobbed quietly from her chair, eyes on the floor, her chorus wide-eyed at her feet.

I tore my gaze away from the enraged Darius to Tabitha and stepped forward to stop her pummeling of Bob, who looked stricken. Laying a hand gently on Tabitha's shoulder, I feared for a moment she would turn her considerable fury on me. When her wet eyes met mine, though, she froze, fist in midair.

I held out my arms. With a sob, she threw herself into my waiting embrace with a metal clink and wept. I cradled my friend as her tough exterior broke. I still didn't know what role she had played in any of this, but I knew her pain. My heart broke for her.

Waves of sorrow shredded her insides. In my mind's eye, I could see the out of control flip of images in her mind as memories assaulted her: Tabitha and Raven as happy toddlers painting pictures, Tabitha and Raven as giggling kindergartners wrapping ribbons around a Maypole, Tabitha and Raven performing a play for a group of adults at a campground. Once happy memories now paired with an even more significant pain of loss.

Then, a young Tabitha weeping, begging to see her friends, asking to see her "aunts and uncles," asking to go to festival again. Her father coldly dismissing her, her mother a silent witness.

"I'm so sorry," I murmured, cradling her in my arms. My vision blurred as her sorrow reached out and dragged me in.

The room quieted until Tabitha's thick sobs and Samantha's soft weeping were all the sounds that lingered.

"Your hometown is like an onion," Gunther told Kyle. The four of us moved to the border of the room away from Tabitha, Samantha, and the chorus. "Peel one layer, and there's another one just underneath."

"This layer gets us closer, sure, but it doesn't answer the big question," Kyle agreed. "Who's behind all this? Do we *really* think a vengeful housewife orchestrated this?"

"Don't dismiss a righteously vengeful woman," Devana told him. "They can be powerful foes."

"Oh, is *that* what you thought you were?" Kyle asked, latching on to yet another opportunity to insult Devana and remind her that he had not forgotten or forgiven.

"Stop it," I snapped at the former detective with a steely glare. "But maybe to the first thing: Darius is a *huge* jerk. If *I* were married to him, *I* might try to break the world open just so I could crush him like a bug in spectacular fashion."

Devana covered a grin with her hand while Kyle and Gunther stared at me, their eyes wide. "What? You don't stare like that at Devana, but *my* comment gets the astonished face?"

"We can try to outrun Devana, at least," Kyle said. "You, not so much. An angry person who can kill with a sustained thought between two beats of a butterfly's wing is a little scarier."

"I don't have to outrun anyone," Gunther shrugged. "I have ringmaster armor. I was just a little surprised my girlfriend had such a vengeful streak."

"Oh, great, thanks," Kyle said, glancing at his watch. "Granted, you and your girlfriend's powers scare me a little bit. The huntress is just a run of the mill attacker."

"If it makes you feel more comfortable to believe that, I'll allow you to," Devana lifted her shoulder in a half shrug. "But you should know, both of you, that you could not outrun me if even the *gods themselves* stepped in to aid you."

Kyle gulped.

"Is this the extent of the conspiracy?" Gunther looked to each of us. "This human melodrama?"

"I'm not satisfied that the Witches' Council isn't involved," I said. I raked my fingers through my hair to pull it out of my face. The dark-haired chorus girl padded around us to grab a candle and pinch it out with her fingers. "But honestly, that's just a feeling. There's nothing here that directly points to it."

"Except timing, motive, outcome," Kyle said as he held up his fingers and counted off. "And Tabitha?"

I shrugged. She didn't know about Raven, but that doesn't mean she wasn't helping her mother.

"Not to mention the fact that they have been quiet, too quiet, while all of this has been going on." Gunther circled back to the Witches' Council. "We are exposed here in the human world, and they are nowhere to be found."

The chorus girl grinned at Gunther as she moved past us. Gunther's eyes darted to the side, and he nodded as the girl returned to Samantha Goodfellow's side.

"Hey, most favored man, eyes over here." My annoyance flared at Gunther's split-second memory of the girl gesticulating on the floor in front of him, and his realization that she smelled of gardenias.

"Sorry," he said, meeting my eyes. "It was an extraordinary thing to encounter. We read about that kind of stuff at the Academy." He reached out to grab my hand. "I never expected I would be greeted as a God anywhere. It was *fascinating*."

"Quit getting distracted. I'll kiss your ankles all you want once we have Samson back."

Gunther flushed.

"The man is not to be trusted," Devana jerked her chin toward Darius, still held against the wall by our lares guard. Poor Bob stared keenly at the still-weeping Tabitha as she laid her head on Samantha's ample chest. The high priestess patted my friend's shoulder and whispered consolingly, while Darius looked at them, his heavy-lidded eyes flashing with irritation. Tabitha forgave the priestess so quickly, and I could feel that it had angered Darius.

The two women ignored him while Melissa continued to whisper fiercely at her lover. I exhaled.

"Yeah, but that's not really news," I told

Devana as I refocused on the conversation. "At least not to us." I looked at Melissa, her finger poking Darius's chest as her mouth ran a mile a minute. Every few seconds she paused, waited for his response, and when he didn't give it, she poked him and started again. "I guess Melissa still has hope for her married boyfriend. Honestly, I thought she was smarter than that."

"Or…not," Kyle said, tilting his head and contemplating the pair.

"What do you mean?"

"That *is* still Michael Hayden's little sister," Kyle gestured, his right eyebrow rising. "Hayden was the first person to tell us about Darius Stevens's criminal inclinations. He insisted that Darius didn't have a wish to topple him until Tabitha knew who and what you were. Melissa Hayden showed up at your parents' house uninvited to bring us to *Il Pirata*."

"*That* young woman seems to put herself in the thick of things, doesn't she?" Devana asked, cocking an eyebrow at me.

"I've never sensed any kind of darkness in her at all," I argued.

"Darkness is not an easy thing for a telepath or empath to sense. It is not an action, a thought, or a feeling. I've met happy sociopaths," Devana countered.

"You *are* a happy sociopath." Kyle spat.

"I'm not always happy," she deadpanned. Kyle coughed and looked away. Devana glanced over at me and winked. I wondered if the two of them were ever going to get over their beef with one another. Well, it really wasn't a beef between the two of them. Kyle couldn't stand Devana, and it seemed Devana was growing tired of worrying about it.

"It's *way* too late for the restaurant to be open," I told the three as I noted the clock on the wall. "If we want to call on Michael Hayden, it will have to wait until morning." My heart sank as I thought of Samson trapped for one more night. "I don't know where he lives."

"I'm sure she does," Kyle pointed at Melissa.

"Guys, *they're* human," I pointed to Tabitha and Samantha, their faces blotchy from crying. "This hit Tabitha like a truck. They need rest. *We* may be able to push without sleep, but they're not going to be able to. And they definitely seem to be a part of this somehow."

"I can magically seal this room," Gunther said as he glanced at the door. "Considering who's in here and who may be outside of here, I'd say it was a good idea to cast some protection. We can all bunk down, get some sleep, and deal with this in the morning."

I hesitantly agreed to my own idea, still thinking of Samson.

CHAPTER 10

THE FOLLOWING MORNING GUNTHER MANIFESTED
a continental breakfast worthy of a budget motel
for the gathered crew of friend and enemy.

The problem was that we still didn't know
which was which.

Tabitha's face was swollen and splotchy, and
she remained on the opposite side of the area
from her father as she ate a bowl of fruity cereal.
She had grown quieter than usual, though I
figured that was to be expected considering what
she had learned.

We had divided to sleep. The members of the
human coven in one part of the room, the true
paranormals in another. Darius and Melissa in a
third area, spurned by everybody.

Bob stood guard, sleepless, over the entire place as we stretched out, protected by Gunther's shield and the Roman's careful attention.

"The place probably opens at 10," I said after taking a bite of an apple. "Are we going to take everyone over there to talk to Hayden?"

"We'd need a bus," Kyle said under his breath. He scanned the room. "I don't see any reason to bring Samantha Goodfellow and those girls. Tabitha, though—"

"I agree, she needs to remain with us," Gunther said.

"Okay, we'll take Tabitha, and—"

"Who put you in charge?" Tabitha asked softly from across the room. Silence fell as people stopped chewing and looked. "I was the one that got captured. This involves members of the coven in practically every way. Even coven secrets," Tabitha said, getting up. "So, I want to know. *Who* put you in charge of deciding for everyone?"

I looked at Tabitha and struggled to keep my face under control.

"Tabitha, dear, don't attack Charlotte," the high priestess told her as she pushed her bulk up to stand beside the sister of her son. "It is *her* familiar that's been taken."

"Yeah, well, he *wouldn't* have been if she hadn't come back to Mickwac, right?" Tabitha pointed out. "If she hadn't come back here, she and her cat and her little cotton candy fantasy land would be completely safe, wouldn't it?"

"I came back because *you* were missing! What's got into you?" I demanded, my face tense.

"A week ago I had normal, run-of-the-mill problems," Tabitha said, her eyes filling with tears even though her voice had an edge like a whetted dagger. "Sure, my gangster hacker dad cheated on my mom. My mom was a drunk, and I believed my best friend had sauntered out of and back into the pages of a legend. But I was handling all that."

"You'll deal with this, too—"

"Oh, god, just *shut up*!" Tabitha shouted. "You're like a one-woman wrecking ball! Aidan's comatose, your cat's been stolen, your boyfriend is so miserable with you he looks like someone kicked his dog every five minutes, and *now* you've knocked over *my* life! Where does it stop?"

"You cannot speak to the ringmaster like that," Bob told her, anguished.

"Oh, and you introduced me to an archaic Roman that has a crush on me!" she said, pointing to Bob. "Will you let him stay here if I like him back? Let me come with you? Regardless, *you'd* be in charge of that decision, right? Not me? Not him?" she demanded, her eyes wild. "You know, Charlotte, there's a *reason* all of this stuff is supposed to stay separate!"

I traded a glance with Gunther.

"What? What are you looking at? Why are you *looking at him*? Can't you even take responsibility for *your own* power? I mean, you wield it like a scythe, don't you? Is that something you do on purpose, or are you just too much of an idiot to keep the people around you from being destroyed? Tell me, *Ringmaster*, are *we* the price for *you*?" Tabitha asked, her cheeks red and her eyes glistening fiercely.

"Child, stop," Samantha said more firmly, her chorus's impassive.

"I'm not a child," Tabitha snapped back without turning around.

"It hurt you as it would wound a child," the high priestess said, her eyes clouded as if she was considering something far off in the distance. "You are angry, like a child. You are furious at your friend for exposing truths in your life that you *long* sensed in the shadows."

Tabitha froze, her eyes still angry. Samantha

went calmly to my friend and spun her tenderly. "Do not shout at the light, child. It can *only* illuminate that which was already there, it can only feed or burn what already exists. Remember your lessons."

Me.

The light.

She must be kidding.

"I have to get out of here," I said, embarrassed that my tone sounded as snotty as it did. I headed toward the back door.

"Charlotte—" Gunther called, stepping forward and lifting his hand.

"Just to the back," I told him. "Just give me a minute. I need some air."

He dropped his hand and bowed.

The backyard was charming. Crystals caught the dawn sunshine, and chimes rang in the Texas breeze passing by. I made my way beyond the herb garden and sat down on a swing bench.

The metal clank reminded me that wherever I went, I was still the ringmaster of the Magical Midway. A reminder that all those around me were unprotected. Except for Gunther.

I didn't blame Tabitha for lashing out at me. Her mind roared all last night as she combed through the past and tried to reorient to the new truths she had confirmed. Her heart ached for Raven, the mysterious young man she had refused repeatedly, but who had only wanted to spend time with her. He interpreted what he felt as attraction and love.

Tabitha now understood it was both less than that, and more profound. A tie of blood that neither one of them knew about because of the lies their parents had told. A lie she had learned the truth of, but which Raven had not.

I peered up at the sun and squinted. What a mess.

The back door opened, and Samantha Goodfellow stepped out. I sighed as the plump woman picked her way through the herbs toward me.

"If I gave you space, you would wallow," she said with a chuckle.

"How can you laugh right now?"

"Even in misery, there is joy," the priestess said. She whomped herself down on the swing with a heave. I clutched the arm and tensed as the bench leaned precariously in her direction.

"She's angry at everyone, even me. But not you," I said as we began to sway. "Why is that?"

"I'm like a comfortable old aunt that was always nice to people," Samantha replied.

"You care about her."

"Of *course* I care about her. I care about *you*, as well."

"You don't know me."

"You don't think some mystery schools knew about the circuses? About your families?" the priestess asked. All traces of levity and humor had vanished from her face. "How do you think *I* knew?"

"I don't know. Books?" I speculated.

"I would bet that there are some humans that know more about you than you know about *yourself*, Charlotte." Samantha looked up at the clear sky and took a deep breath. "You all just accept that which you are and that which is around you. Without question."

"Well, sure," I shrugged, puzzled. "Doesn't everyone?"

"For us, magic and myth is something we have lost. We will paw through the soil and call out to the stars hoping to experience for a *second* what we recognize we *had* once. We will examine lines in a book, plants in a garden, the pattern of waves in the sea just to understand a fraction of what *you* take for granted."

"You mean human witches?"

"I mean *humans*."

We fell silent, swinging.

"You remind me of Ms. Elkins," I told her after a few minutes. "Well, without the grumpiness."

"The norn?" she asked. I shifted and stared. "I told you. Some of us know more about you than you know yourselves. The nornir are fearsome women, but presumptuous. When so many in the world believe in free will, they cling to the idea of destiny."

"You don't believe in fate?"

"I believe. And the world believes. So the world goes as we believe," she said as if chanting a poem. "If you believe in fate, then fate binds you. If you do not, thus, it does not."

I thought about it, then thought about it again, and then shook my head. "I don't understand what you mean."

"Thoughts are energy. Magic is power. And right now you and Gunther hold much of it. The Witches' Council holds more," Samantha smiled. "If any of you ever *use* it, you *may* shake the world. Or," she shrugged, "you could empower it. At some point, it will be your choice."

"Why does everybody keep saying that?"

"Perhaps when you figure that out, you'll have your answer," Samantha said as she tapped my hand. Pushing herself up, she tottered back toward the house.

Leaving me even more confused than before.

"*That* was mysterious," Gunther said as he sat down on the bench. Sliding over, he lifted his arm and put it around my shoulder.

"You were listening?" He nodded. I shrugged. "What *isn't* cryptic these days? Anyway, I couldn't tell. That you were in there, I mean. You don't talk in my head much anymore."

"Yeah, that's one reason I wanted to come out here."

"Did our connection break or go wonky or something?" I asked. I pulled up my hand to check the ring. The lawgiver ring, the thing that bonded me telepathically with Gunther, was still bright gold, shiny, and wedded to my skin somehow. I sighed in relief. "Not black, so I'm still a good person. I got worried there for a second. I figured maybe Tabitha was right, and the ring had turned against me because all of this actually *is* my fault."

He held up his hand, and his ring shone bright gold in the sun. I reached out and threaded my hand through his.

"Tabitha's just lashing out, you know that," Gunther said. "I recognize it, frankly. I think I've been doing a little lashing out of my own."

"What do you mean?"

"I just watched what hidden truths did to Tabitha when they were brought to light," Gunther told me as we swung gently together hand in hand. "So, let's just say that I *haven't* been as straightforward with you as I should have been, and leave it at that. I am sorry if anything I said or did hurt you."

I waited. After about thirty seconds, I tilted my head.

He smiled back.

I waited another thirty seconds.

He was silent.

"And?" I asked.

"That's it," he smiled.

That's it? Gunther was sorry for not being straightforward with me, but he wasn't going to follow up on what it was he wasn't candid about?

Sheesh.

Men.

"So, honey," I chirped, struggling to keep my frustration from spilling out into my words. "I have noticed you *seemed* to be hiding something. You've been quiet. In here," I pointed to my head. "And here," I said as I brushed his lip lightly. "What is it?" I asked brightly, willing my smile to shine from my eyes.

Even though I felt like whacking him with the trowel laying just two feet in front of us.

Gunther clutched my hand with a squeeze. Then pain darkened his eyes. He turned his face away, releasing my hand.

"*Don't* you do that," I demanded, reaching up to turn his face back toward me. My eyes searched his. "Talk to me. *Tell* me what's going on. I thought we were in this together?"

He touched my cheek, his eyes seeking mine as his thumb toyed with my hair. It was a romantic scene, sitting with my boyfriend in this beautiful garden, the creak of the wood as we swung gently. I should feel secure, comfortable, but I didn't.

I felt dread.

"We are not," Gunther said as he sighed.

I blinked.

Okay, I thought he might say something I

didn't want to hear, but *we weren't in this together*? I wasn't expecting him to say that at all. My breathing became shallow as the fear took hold.

My mind raced.

Oh my gosh.

Was he breaking up with me?

He dropped his hand from my cheek and got up. I stayed silent, waiting, swinging, panicking. He had to know what I was thinking and the longer he said nothing, the more freaked out I became. He faced the shop for several more moments and then without looking at me, he spoke.

"I'm alone, Charlotte. I'm *alone*, and I miss you and them. I am also jealous of you for what you have that I don't. Even a little resentful. And I feel *terrible* about that. I feel terrible that I am…I am envious of you."

Wait, what?

Them? Who's *them*?

As if a bolt of insight suddenly struck my brain, I remembered what Tabitha had told me back at the bungalow. That his mother and his father lived in my circus because the Witches' Council had barred Gerda Makepeace from her family's home when she died. Anna Makepeace,

Gunther's new spectral adopted sister, *also* lived at my circus. *I* lived at my circus.

I had everything.

It didn't really feel like it, but I did.

I had everything.

Everything except him.

"Gunther, I am *so* sorry," I whispered and hopped off the swing.

What a jerk I'd been.

I had never stopped to think about the fact that everyone Gunther had been close to was at the Magical Midway, with me. Even after Tabitha explained it to me, I shunted it all aside to be dealt with later. Then I forgot about it.

Guilt stung me.

"It's not your fault," he said as he turned and hugged me. "I know I shouldn't be envious, but I can't help it. I have learned to do so much since I was elevated *because* of my loneliness and isolation. But even so—I can't figure out how to fix this. I just don't know how to change it."

"We'll figure it out," I told him. He nodded, but the suffering that radiated from his face seemed permanently etched there. "We will!"

"Maybe," he whispered, and then he kissed me. "I wish we could just join the circuses permanently. Then we would never have to be apart, and I could see my family more often. It would solve everything."

I sighed and leaned into him with a loud clank.

Solve everything. That would be nice.

However, it sounded like a tall order.

I couldn't even get my darn cat back.

CHAPTER 11

THE ROOM WAS MUTED. TABITHA'S FACE WAS LINED with hostility, lines that grew even sharper as she glanced at me. I struggled to meet her gaze with as neutral a look on my face as possible.

When she rolled her eyes and looked away, I knew I apparently needed to practice my poker face a little more.

"Okay, so let's figure out what we're going to do this morning," I said after Gunther and I came back into the room. I was risking Tabitha's wrath by taking charge, but someone had to get us moving. And it was my cat missing, after all.

"Gunther and I will talk to Michael Hayden. Melissa, if you'd come with us—" I spun and peered around for Hayden's sister. "Melissa? Where's Melissa?"

Tabitha looked at me from her cross-legged perch on a table. "She left with my father."

"Wait, what do you mean, she *left*?"

"I mean the two of them saw the open door," Tabitha drawled, pointing to the right. "They stood up on their own two legs, walked toward the door, opened it, and walked through." Tabitha walked her fingers along her palm as if she was interpreting for a child. "I imagine after they were through the door, they got a cab somewhere."

"Why didn't you stop them?" I asked Bob.

"I can't take action against the humans," he reminded me. "I can't even slow their ability to leave, Ringmaster."

"But you stood guard over us all night!"

"I did," he nodded, smiling proudly. "My job is to watch over you."

"But if you can't take action against the humans, what would you have done if someone human attacked us?"

"Woken you up so you and Gunther could handle it. Obviously. I mean, it's your rule. Well, and the Witches' Council rule. But *mostly* your rule."

This gig.

There were times I hated this gig.

"Charlotte, he remarked that he was running to his office to get something," Samantha Goodfellow said as she stood up and strode over to us. The high priestess looked like she'd spent a sleepless night tossing and turning in her bedroll, though her chorus sounded refreshed and well-rested.

"Samantha, I've meant to ask you, who are—" I began, but the ensemble leader cut me off.

"Ringmaster," the girl breathed, sprinting toward me. "Maybe we should go over all the facts you know so far about Samson? Perhaps we can help you figure out whether it's safe to go there and who might be behind the capture of your familiar."

"Well, we *know* who's behind it," I said, leaning against a chair. "Tabitha's mother and Raven. Tabitha's mother kidnapped Samson from the Magical Midway, and when we went to investigate at Sarah's home, we overheard Raven speaking to her. So, we know your high priestess's son—"

"My brother," Tabitha cut in.

"We didn't know *that* at the time," I said. "He's working with Sarah to hold Samson and try to steal the Magical Midway's power. What his underlying motive is beyond the obvious, if there even is one, though, we don't know."

The chorus stared at me attentively, eyes wide, nodding as I spoke. I studied the three young women again, eyes narrowing as I considered them. Why didn't I know their names? We'd slept overnight with them in the store/ritual room of Avalon Grove. They'd overheard countless things that humans really shouldn't be listening to.

And yet I did not understand who the young women were, or what their names were.

"Pardon me, but your na—" Gunther began, but again, like magic, someone spoke and thwarted the culmination of the question.

"So, explain why we want to talk to Michael Hayden, then?" one of the chorus, the quiet brunette, asked.

"Michael Hayden and Darius Stevens are both criminals," I clarified. "Darius is sleeping with Melissa Hayden, Michael's sister, and Melissa's showed up in the middle of this a few times uninvited."

"So?" she tilted her head. "What does this have to do with your cat?"

"What does this have to do with my cat?" I mused out loud as I tried to recall why, exactly, we had delayed rescuing Samson just to speak to Michael Hayden. "Oh, right! So…no, that's not it…Yes, um, Michael Hayden could be involved in this!"

"How?" she asked as the loud raven-haired girl, the one I had assumed was the leader of the chorus, glared at her. Gunther's eyes narrowed.

"Well, you see—" I began, but Gunther's hand reached out to settle lightly on my arm. I listened for his voice in my head, but there was only silence. What is he concerned about that he's afraid to even think to me? "We don't know," I said, ending the statement abruptly.

Tabitha snorted.

"This seems like a rude question after we've spent so much time together, but what are your names?" I asked hurriedly, a little shocked that I got the full question out of my mouth before someone spoke and derailed me again.

"Oh, my, look at the time!" the chorus head shouted. "Our Dad will be so upset with us for staying out all night. Come on!" With a smile and an energetic wave, the raven-haired beauty led the two brunettes out the door. The first two flounced out.

The quiet brunette stopped in the doorway and turned. "You are running out of time," she breathed so the two women in front of her wouldn't be able to hear. My eyes locked on hers, and it felt like the air had been sucked from my lungs.

"*What* just happened?" I murmured to myself. My head felt like it was refocusing. I knew where I had felt this slight realignment before.

At the Werebear Jamboree.

As the glamour wore off.

"*Who* were those women?" Gunther asked Samantha Goodfellow sharply. He rubbed his eyes. Bob looked bewildered as Kyle came out of an adjoining bathroom, his hair wet, and inspected the room.

"Just members of my coven," she said, startled at the tone in Gunther's ordinarily soft and gentle voice. "Just girls from the local college, I think."

"And their names?" I demanded after I drew a deep, shuddering breath.

"Their names are…they are…well, *that's* just odd," Samantha said, her eyes burning with concentration. Her muscles were tense—as if trying to dig through her brain to find the names of the three women was a monumental effort. "You know, I just can't recall, precisely."

"Just stop trying," I told her, waving a dismissive hand in her direction. "You won't be able to. I doubt they ever told you."

"The Witches' Council," Tabitha told her.

"How do *you* know that?" I asked with more wariness than I meant to.

"There's three of them, right?" Tabitha asked, rising up. "There were three here. No one can remember what their names were. Priestess, do you even remember how they got here? How long they've been coming to the coven? Who brought them here?"

Samantha's face grew red as she tried to turn her brain inside out and shake loose the information she wanted to know. Beads of perspiration sprang to her plump face. With an explosive gasp, she collapsed into a chair. "This is *absurd!*" she declared. "How did I circle with three girls that I *don't even know?*"

"They glamoured you," Tabitha said, kneeling down to reassure the woman. Despite everything Tabitha had found out in the past day, it was clear that she held a sincere devotion to the portly priestess. "It wasn't your fault."

"Oh, all of this is my fault," Samantha wailed

and pressed her hands to her cheeks. Tabitha sprang to the priestess's side. Kyle stood quietly behind them watching everything keenly. "I should ask the huntress witch to yank out my heart for being such a senseless old fool!"

"Devana wouldn't do that, even if you asked. Would you, Devana?" I turned to locate the huntress witch and realized that she, too, was no longer in the room. "Okay, where the heck is *she*, now? And how did I not notice that, like, *everyone* was missing?"

"I'm still here, boss," Bob proclaimed pridefully, his eyes still glued to Tabitha as she soothed the priestess.

"I know, Bob, thanks," I saluted.

"You know it," he saluted back without tearing his eyes from my human friend.

"That answers our question about the Witches' Council being involved," Gunther said with a gesture to Kyle. "You didn't notice people were gone because a glamour can mess with your perceptions. Glamours are nasty business, and there were three going on in here. I, uh, even contained the magic with the shield last night," he pointed out sheepishly. "That probably made it stronger."

"It doesn't answer our question *about* them

being involved," I told him as we leaned in and formed a close circle. "It answers the question about whether they *know*. Okay, they *realize what's going on*. The real question is, are they observers or are they instigators?"

"Does it matter?" Kyle asked.

"It matters," Gunther told Kyle.

"If they're instigators? Something really, exceedingly bad is awaiting us at the cavern," I said glancing over to Samantha and Tabitha on the other side of the room. "If they're observers, we just have to worry about the human's attack capabilities. Not theirs."

"Either way, these humans are in trouble." Kyle followed my gaze over to Tabitha and Samantha. "They won't let them live past whatever their agenda is here. They know too much."

CHAPTER 12

"Do you remember Tabitha talking to her father last night at all?" I asked Gunther, my voice low so the group walking toward the entrance to *Il Pirata* wouldn't hear. "I remember her yelling at him when the information about Raven first came out, but I don't think I saw them talk ever again."

"No, he just sat on the side of the room, Melissa whispering away at him," Gunther said. We paused by the truck. He was frowning as he watched Tabitha and Bob, Bob's muscled arm casually resting on the small of her back. "Have you made up your mind about her?"

"Who?"

"Tabitha," Gunther lifted his chin in the pair's

direction, Kyle beside them glancing back at us. The centaur was sticking close to the questionable couple, closer than he ordinarily would if Bob was escorting someone. "Do *you* think she's part of this?"

"I think everybody is part of this," I said carefully, all the convoluted information passing through my mind. "The paranormal world and the human one. The Witches' Council. The human coven. Our circus."

"As it were a wheel in the middle of a wheel," he muttered. His gaze sharpened and settled on Tabitha. I chuckled softly. "What? Did I say something?"

"We say 'wheels within wheels' now."

"The human testament book expresses it more poetically."

"That's probably true, but it's old. That's why they call it the *Old* Testament."

"You're not answering the question," Gunther observed. He grasped my hand to draw me into his arms. "You seem tired, love." Shivering despite the pleasant morning sunlight, I sighed. I'd never tire of hearing him call me that. It was like something out of a storybook. "How are you managing?"

"I'm concerned about Samson. I'm confused

about what, exactly, is going on here. I'm tired," I admitted as I relaxed my head on his shoulder. "But I'm glad you're here. I think you're keeping me sane."

He drew his head back to look at me. "Oh? How so?"

"Just by being here."

He grinned. "That's nice of you to say, love." Gunther kissed the tip of my nose with a slight clink.

"I don't know; it's strange," I said as we remained together in the parking lot. "I feel like I *should* freak out. When did the Witches' Council showing up just become, like, *an ordinary* thing? Being glamoured, not being able to trust my own eyes, my own impressions. When did that become *routine*?"

Gunther took a minute before he responded, but when he spoke, his observation had a ring of truth that made me uncomfortable. "Perhaps you're finally one of us. Maybe it's taken all this time for you to trust what our world is."

If he was right, the world was now shifting sands of deception punctuated by full-on attacks. No amount of cotton candy and circus peanuts could put a shine on that reality.

"You and I were going to change the world," I

said, pulling back and thinking about our plans to overthrow the Witches' Council, remake the paranormal world into a kinder, more democratic one. "Do you think none of the things we planned will happen? That there's just...I don't know what to call it. Apathetic acceptance of the status quo? We haven't done any work on that in such a long time."

"I think you have to understand something to effect change—I mean, that's the core of magic, right? Except for us. Ringmasters don't have to understand *anything*. There are structures built within the power itself so any fool could wield it, and probably adequately."

"When you put it like that, we sound horrible," I protested, but Gunther just snickered.

"We *are* dreadful, Charlotte. We're also crucial. Maggie and Eiggam are two sides of a conflict. If one prevails, the other's energy doesn't *dissipate*. The champion will absorb the loser's energy, but their perspective? Their gift?"

"Yes?"

"They convert it. The winner becomes twice as strong, twice as dominant. The loser's viewpoint, their gift—*that* goes away. That energy, though, becomes the bounty of the vi—"

"That's *it*," I cut him off, thrusting him away.

"What's it?"

"That's why the Witches' Council is here. Think about it." I began pacing in front of the truck. "If Samantha Stevens gets my energy? You don't have a ringmaster. You have a human being with powers they don't understand and *no guardian anymore*."

"I don't follow you."

I paced and thought. Paced and thought. Paced and thought. Then I turned to him again.

"Why do *we* have a guardian and *you* don't?" I asked him, surprised no one had ever asked that question before. "Why can I be taken down by the kidnapping of a snarky cat and you *can't*?"

The circuses all ran more or less identically. One ringmaster, a dome of energy that protected the inhabitants inside. The same rules, more or less. At least on the big things.

But *one* Samson. *One* guardian.

Why?

"No one knew that you did. *You* told me about him," Gunther said, shifting on his feet. "Since you have, though, I've never really understood that."

"What if *we* have a guardian," I said, pointing back and forth to the two of us. "What if Samson *isn't* just the guardian of the Magical Midway?

What if he's like, I don't know, the fulcrum point for *all* of Maggie's energy? All of it, meaning *all* the circuses?"

Gunther froze.

"Think about it. Why would *our* circus alone out of all the circuses have some super-powered pet? What did Samson say to me when your dad died? Before you became ringmaster? Do you remember?" I looked at him, my eyebrow lifted.

"*We are vulnerable*," Gunther whispered.

"*We*. Not *your* circus. Not you. Not *my* circus. And why would *my* circus be vulnerable because *your* dad died?" I asked, my hands animatedly waving in the air. "He wasn't our ringmaster. Technically, he had *nothing* to do with us. I could have broken that link between the circuses in a flat second. But no—*we* were vulnerable."

Gunther leaned on the SUV's hood for support. He looked like he might pass out.

"They're coming for us, Gunther. Right here in Mickwac."

"Both of us," Gunther breathed.

"All of us," I corrected.

∽

My mind was racing as I stormed past our three companions at the entry and burst into the *Il Pirata* restaurant. Checking the room for Michael Hayden, I spotted the dapper mob boss leaning over a table of less dapper thugs eating eggs.

"You and I need to talk," I said after loudly stomping over to the sketchy group. Kyle, who followed my aggressive beeline across the quaint eatery, looked dumbfounded at the dramatic change in my attitude. "Find someplace private. Now."

Hayden frowned and carefully took stock of me. Then his eyes wandered over those of my companions he could see. Turning back, he said, "I am not accustomed to anybody approaching me in such a manner."

The thugs at the table looked ready to brandish their forks in defense of their boss.

"You claim to know what I am," I warned him quietly. I stepped forward, so close that he could probably feel the breath of my words on his skin. "If you know what I am, you know what I can do. I don't care what you're accustomed to. In the rear. Now."

I knocked Michael Hayden off balance with my words. I could tell. His eyes flashed left and right as if looking for an escape, but then he waved once and turned, gesturing for us to follow.

I'd be amazed if *anyone* had ever spoken to the man the way I just, had considering what a brutal psychopath he was, but even if I couldn't magic up an attack spell? I was *reasonably* sure my metal-clanky armor would hurt a whole lot if I flung my arm into his head hard enough.

"Where's my sister, Melissa?" Hayden asked as he swung to confront me in his private office. It was a dark place, lined with dark wood shelves that held decorative bottles and pitchers of all shapes and sizes. Directly behind his desk was the largest and most elaborate, interspersed with boxes of discolored brass. "I haven't seen or spoken to her since you all came for your little dinner the other night."

"Do you know that your sister has been sleeping with *Darius Stevens*? For months?"

The fury that passed across his face would have naturally led me to believe, under normal circumstances, that he didn't know. In *these* circumstances, though, he could just be ticked off that I found out.

My telepathy, empathy failed me on sociopaths—and sociopathic crazy people were becoming an all too common thing in my world.

Both worlds.

"What do you want, Astley? Did you really come here to confer with me regarding my sister's sex life?" he challenged me coldly.

"My cat. That's what I started out wanting, and that's what I want now."

"Have you tried the animal shelter?" he inquired amiably, a false smile on his face.

I stepped forward and raised my arm, fully prepared to test my theory about my magically-armored-arm-as-lead-pipe, when Gunther reached forward and held me steady. The room resounded with the uneasy breathing of all present, and it felt hot with a crackling energy of scarcely veiled animosity.

Except for Hayden, of course.

That man was cold as ice.

"Are you involved in her cat's disappearance?" Kyle asked. I tingled with indignation. "Who your sister sleeps with isn't any of our business—"

"Speak for yourself," Tabitha snapped at Kyle.

"Ah, the young Ms. Stevens," Michael smiled coldly as he spotted Tabitha for the first time behind Bob. "You look *remarkably* angry for someone rescued by such a lively troupe of mythological creatures. You must be *thrilled* that your former friend possessed the necessary powers to pluck you from your underwater prison."

"Bite me," she snapped again while Bob pressed his arm against her.

"And yet I sense that your rescue and reunion was not all you hoped it would be."

Tabitha returned his observation with silence.

Hayden glanced at Bob, then his eyes skipped to the Roman's arm intimately wrapped around Tabitha. A second later, he pinned me with his eyes and smiled.

"Gathered friends," Hayden flung his arms wide and put his friendly mask firmly back in place. "I don't have a cat, don't want a cat, and am quite allergic to cats. So, you see, unless you want a fabulous Italian brunch? Your trip here has been *utterly* wasted. Tortes all around, then?"

"Actually, I'd kinda like a torte," Bob said.

I whipped around and glared at the lares.

"No torte?" he asked, slumping with disappointment.

"I don't think so." I turned back around.

"Oh?" Michael Hayden raised his eyebrow at me.

"How d'you know where we found Tabitha?" I asked him.

"Pardon me?"

"You said you hadn't seen your sister since we were here for dinner," I pointed out. "The police don't know where Tabitha was found, just that she was—it's not like we could explain it. Right? So, *that* begs the question—*how* do you know about her underwater prison?"

Hayden's face was impassive except for a slight twitch in his right eye.

"Did you know where she was the whole time? Or just after the fact?"

Silence.

Tabitha's face was a kaleidoscope of confusion, anxiety, and resentment. She glared across the room at the brother of her outer-court coven mate. Her eyes bored into the criminal mastermind, but aside from a veiled glance here and there, his eyes fixed on me.

"I have nothing more to say to you, Astley," Michael Hayden said after a long silence.

"I imagine you wouldn't," Gunther said, his head tilting. "You mortals aren't much better than the Witches' Council. I had always thought that with so many more experiences, so much more opportunity, so much more to learn that…that you all would have matured further than we had. I was mistaken. You are *no* better than us."

Gunther's observation had been delivered in

the most even, startlingly sympathetic tone, considering what he said and his clear intent in verbalizing it. For a moment, I was embarrassed —embarrassed by humankind, ashamed that the man I loved was so clearly disapproving of the place I still thought of as my home.

"You know, we're not perfect—" Kyle said, clearly offended at the attack on the town he once called home, too, but Michael Hayden cut the centaur off and seethed at Gunther.

"*Brilliant* observation coming from a witch that uses his immeasurable power to make *horses prance in a circle*," Hayden said, obviously insulted and intending to strike back just as hard. "You dare to talk to *me* about evolution? We have to work for our authority. We overcome difficulties you can't even imagine—"

"And you somehow think we don't?" I asked him.

"They give you the world, and you spend your leadership to make cotton candy and unicorns!" Michael sneered. "So casual about death I doubt you've thought once about the djinn!"

That hurt. "Of course I've thought about Jeannie!" I argued, but...had I?

Had I thought about her at all since we sent the Magical Midway off? Or Uncle Phil and how he was faring? There was just *so much* going on, though. So much to deal with at once. The rest of the folks here didn't know her that well, but...I did.

"They can't make unicorns."

"*What?*" Hayden turned to Bob and glared at him sharply.

"The ringmasters. They can't *make* unicorns. Magic can't *create* a sentient being, and unicorns are sentient beings," Bob pointed out, gesturing to Gunther and me. "They *can* make cotton candy, though. That point? That was a valid point." Bob nodded earnestly. "The unicorns, though? Not really. Not a good point. That's all."

Michael Hayden worked to keep his expression cold, calculated, and sociopathic, but he couldn't wholly disguise his astonishment at the inappropriate timing of Bob's conclusion. Tabitha smiled and leaned into the clownish warrior.

"You're lares, aren't you?" Hayden asked Bob. Bob nodded. "How old are you?"

"Oh, I don't know, a millennium?" Bob said ambiguously (and inaccurately). "Maybe two. I don't think three, though." His eyes scanned the ceiling as if the exact sum of years would be written up there. Then he shrugged and beamed at the sociopath. "I don't know. A long time. We're kind of immortal, apparently."

"Unthinkable. An idiot like *that* has immortality," Hayden murmured. He turned and picked up a piece of paper, crumpled it up, and threw it away into a blue and white trash a bag hanging off a drawer handle.

"He has a purpose, and it's a purpose of service. Maybe if *you* had a purpose of service someone would grant you a few extra years," I told him.

"I *have* a purpose of service," he answered, leaning back against his desk and crossing his arms. "I serve *myself*. It's the only service that matters."

"If you only serve *yourself*, why did you even *offer* us tortes?" Bob asked Hayden. The rest of us turned to stare at him. "That's just wrong, dude. You don't tease tortes," the lares mumbled, shaking his head.

CHAPTER 13

"I just...It's...Argh!" I said, pacing the parking lot. Gunther and Kyle stood watching me, while Tabitha's back flexed with tension as she leaned against Bob. "I just want to hit someone. I swear I feel like just—"

"Get yourself under control," Kyle said softly, his eyes tracking me with unease. "Take a deep breath, lie down on the ground if you have to, Charlotte. But center your thoughts, breathe."

I sucked in the clean Texas air and tried to will myself to calm down. Kyle was right, losing it would only make matters worse, and if I hit the truck in frustration? I stood a good chance of taking out the engine.

"I just feel like the world's running at us," I

protested. I hurled myself gently against the truck with a clank and crossed my arms. The force was enough to dent the front panel and make me feel marginally better. "It's like juggling knives while simultaneously having them thrown at you."

"Oh, for goodness' sake, Charlotte," Tabitha mumbled into Bob's chest from the other side of the vehicle. "I wish you would just shut up,"

"What?" I asked.

Tabitha didn't respond.

I slammed my hand lightly on the metal to get her attention. "What did you say to me?" Gunther pulled me back away from my parents' SUV before he had to magic them up another one.

Tabitha continued to ignore me.

"If you have something to say to me, Tabitha, just come out and say it!" I demanded, raising my hand again.

"What did you *think* would happen when you became the most *powerful being in the entire world?* That you'd get to watch movies and chill because you didn't need to work? Have time to read? Take a vacation?" Tabitha said as she pivoted around. "That you'd get to just stay in your little corner of the world and be left alone?"

"Well…" I hesitated.

"You didn't even think about it, did you?"

Tabitha glanced at Gunther. "And you...you knew that this would be your life since you were an infant. You should be prepared for this."

"I did," Gunther answered her calmly. "What's happening now, however, is much more than anyone expected."

"Why?" she asked, her head tilting. "*Why* is it more than you expected? *How* many circuses were there originally? And you two are the only two left? And that's been happening for a hundred years or more?"

Tabitha wordlessly held out her arms, her bitter expression still hopeful that Gunther would understand what she was trying to say.

"Perhaps we should have seen it, but we didn't. Our forefathers didn't, and Charlotte and I didn't, either."

"I'd like to remind all of you that Hayden has this parking lot bugged," Kyle interrupted. "Do we really want to get into a conversation about this here? Especially when we strongly believe that he's wrapped up in this?"

"*Your secrets* is how all this started," Tabitha told Kyle.

"Mine?" Kyle asked, surprised.

"No, not you, specifically—this." Tabitha waved her hands at all of us. "All of you. Tucked in a corner. Hidden. Apart. Yet you all run around like you're *way* more significant than we are. Like you *matter* more."

"The Witches' Council thinks they're more important than *everybody*," I argued. "It's not just the humans they look down upon. It's the werebears, the circus witches, my parents residing in the human world, families working outside of Imperatorial City—"

"You can heal people, right?" Tabitha asked, turning to Gunther, and cutting me off mid-sentence. "You made it so Melissa Hayden could walk again, right?"

"How did you know that?" Kyle asked her. Gunther remained stoic and silent.

"Do I *look* like an idiot?" Tabitha glared at Kyle and raked her hand to pull her hair from her face. When Kyle didn't respond, she turned back. "Well, Gunther?"

He nodded an affirmative answer. "What is your point, Tabitha?" Gunther's question was without accusation, without judgment, and his eyes searched hers intently.

"About three hours toward the coast there's a children's hospital with little kids, *lots* of little kids, dying of all sorts of injuries and diseases,"

she told him angrily. "You ever gone there?" He
nodded no. "You ever *thought* of going there?"

Gunther looked troubled.

I took a deep breath.

"Tabitha, we're not gods—"

"*Aren't* you?" she asked me, a deeper frown
etching her face.

"Of course not!" I took a step back, but I
wasn't really sure why I did. Instinctively, I
wanted to put distance between her words
and me.

"Think about that a little more before you
deny it, Charlotte," Tabitha said as Michael
Hayden, his face white, came dashing out of the
restaurant.

"Oh, great. Now what?" I muttered.

His pace wasn't casual; his expression was full of
shock and skepticism. I almost wished I had a
camera and could snap a picture.

He looked *barely* sociopathic.

"You healed my sister." Hayden stepped up
and confronted me. I shook my head no. "Who,
then? Who's responsible for the fact that she can

walk? *One* of you is. I heard you over the speaker," he said, gesturing toward Tabitha. "Tell me!"

There was a moment of silence as everyone refused to answer, and then Gunther's voice buzzed in my mind. *Do I admit it was me?*

You may as well. I feel like everyone knows everything, anyway. Maybe he'll help us if he knows it was you.

"I am," Gunther said. He forced himself off the truck and stood up to face the man. The two stared at one another as we watched. After what seemed like an eternity, Michael Hayden held his hand out toward Gunther to shake.

My boyfriend looked down, sighed, and shook the murderer's hand.

"I owe you," Michael Hayden breathed, his face twisted with frustration. As if owing Gunther anything was the last thing the man needed today.

"If you owe him, maybe you could tell us where the cat is," I asked. Hayden snorted.

"Nice try. I said I owed *him*. Not you. It's not *his* cat."

There he is. There's the psychotic narcissist I know.

I opened my mouth to argue with him, but closed it hurriedly. So far, no one but Gunther

and I knew what I believed about Samson.
Hayden clearly didn't record his surveillance or,
if he did, he hadn't listened to the previous
conversation, if it had, in fact, been caught on his
microphones.

"What does that mean in *your* world?"
Gunther asked him sincerely, his face curious.
"You owing me something, I mean. Is it a pledge,
an obligation?"

"It's a debt. If in the future you need
something from me, you have only to ask, and I
will be there. Only *once*, so choose carefully. You
don't get a do-over."

"Are you allowed to decline?" Gunther's head
shifted.

"He is," I answered. "He's making the
agreement. He can break it if he wants, so I
wouldn't count on him."

"Okay, *goddess*," Tabitha's voice was level, but a
trace of sarcasm leaked through. I turned, and she
raised her eyebrow.

"Your girlfriend's conclusion is technically
correct, but I keep my commitments. It may be a
distinct sense of honor, but it is *mine*," he said
earnestly. The two men looked into one
another's eyes, and Gunther finally gave him a
nod. "So be it, then." Hayden turned away

without a formal farewell and walked back to his restaurant.

"I don't know if that's a good or a bad thing," I said, hitching my head in the departing mobster's direction.

"I think we need a case board to keep track of all this stuff." Kyle rubbed his chin. "We need to go back to one of the circuses and find a quiet place to sort through all of this. Somewhere we can't be overheard."

I closed my eyes as the frustration bubbled up in me again. I didn't even have to ask him why. The Council was somewhere in town, and they could be anyone. Maybe even anything. We didn't know who or what we could trust. I knew he was right, but I was tired of the delays.

"We should also check on Aidan," I agreed.

"What about Devana?" Gunther asked. "We don't even know where she went."

"She can take care of herself in *any* realm," Kyle said as he strode toward the driver's side of the truck. "She knows where Charlotte's parents live. If she needs us, they can signal us via cauldron."

~

I clambered into the backseat with Gunther and rested my head on his shoulder. Though I missed my yurt and circus, part of me didn't want to travel back to the Magical Midway yet. I hadn't honestly had to deal with Jeannie's death or my uncle's despair over her loss, and I didn't want to. It was one more thing on top of a pile of things that started to feel overwhelming.

"Oh, my love," Gunther whispered, his arm wrapping around me more tightly. "I wish I could take these burdens from you."

"You *have* half of these burdens," Tabitha called from the seat behind us where she sat cuddled in Bob's embrace. Any distance there had been between them disappeared as Tabitha's own issues began to pile up. "You're a ringmaster, too. I genuinely don't get why you guys genuflect to *her* so much."

"You know, I'm *literally* right here listening to you," I said. I sat up and turned around in the bench seat to stare at her resentful face. "Don't talk about me like I'm not here."

"Don't tell me what to do like I'm one of your chattel," Tabitha spat back. Bob reached out to pat her arm.

"Chattel! Chattel? What the hell is that supposed to mean?" I exploded. "I get you're going through a tough time at the moment, but I don't know why you've decided to hold me responsible for all of it!" I was seething with fury at the constant barrage of attacks from my former friend. An old friend that was looking guiltier and guiltier by the minute.

"You honestly can't tell, *your highness?*"

It was unsettling to see Tabitha go from a brusque but caring person to someone that spat venom, judgment, and bitterness at every opportunity. "Maybe I should have just left you down in that grotto," I said wearily. I spun away and settled back into Gunther with a clank. "I probably would have my cat back at this point if I didn't have to deal with all your drama."

A louder, stronger clank echoed in my head.

Then another, even louder one.

"What the heck are you doing?" I shouted as I whipped around.

"Hitting you on the head," Tabitha said, grinning wickedly. She reached out and smacked me, my cheek clanging with a deep metal echo. "It's very cathartic, if you want to know the truth. It may not hurt—but that's *gotta* be annoying."

Clank.

"Stop it!"

"Make me," she challenged. Clank. Another clank.

"Bob, stop her!" I ordered the lares.

Bob looked from me to Tabitha and back to me again. Then he smiled at me with a shrug. "She's a human being. And she can't really hurt you, you know," he said. "And I can't really hurt her because, you know, *rules*. So, everything's all good, boss. See? Nothing to worry about."

"Has everyone lost their minds?" I shrieked as Tabitha rained an outpouring of clanking smacks to my head, face, shoulders, and arms. "*Quit hitting me!*"

She raised her face to laugh at me, her palms smacking against me with such ferocity and pressure that I sang like a steelpan on a Caribbean beach. With a yell, I rose and drew my hand back—

Gunther sprang to action and grabbed my arm. Bob threw his body across Tabitha's to protect her from my strike before I did any damage to her delicate human flesh and blood with my frustrating loss of control.

Tabitha peeked at me over Bob's shoulder, her face turned up defiantly as if my action was *precisely* the response she had been trying to provoke all along.

"I wouldn't have done it," I whispered, alarmed at my own urge. An urge that once would have been a rough shove but could now be a fatal blow. My hands shook, Gunther's hands still clasped lightly around my wrist.

"And you're afraid of *us*?" she asked, her voice barely above a whisper. "No one should have this kind of capability, Charlotte. *No one should have this much power.* But if you're going to have it? Someone will always want to take it from you."

I exhaled forcefully as Gunther relaxed his grip.

"You *are* a goddess," she said as I sank down on the seat, my eyes glued to hers. "You *just are.* Whether you should be? Whether *anyone* should be?" she paused. "That's another question altogether."

CHAPTER 14

WE ALL TRAIPSED LOUDLY THROUGH MY PARENTS' house toward the back veranda. As I arrived at the screen door to follow, I snapped my fingers and turned to drop the keys for the truck back in the dish beneath the kitchen phone where my parents kept them.

"Charlotte!" my mother gasped, unable to hide her shock at my expression when I practically smacked into her. "You look *frightful*, what's happened?

"Nothing more than usual," I waved my hand in a dismissal of my mother and turned away to exit out the back. Then I halted, my rubber-soled shoes squeaking on her immaculately clean kitchen floor as she flung her emotional injury back at me. I half-turned and met my mother's surprised eyes. "I'm sorry. I didn't mean to do that."

"Dismiss the woman that labored hours upon hours to bring you into this world?" Mom asked, her eyebrow so far up her forehead I thought it would reach her hairline. "No, I didn't think you did. Sit down, let me get you something to eat—"

"I can't, we have to get back to the circus," I told her, my palm flat against the half-open screen door.

"A cold drink, then."

"I can't, I have to—"

"Sit," she pointed at the chair.

"Mom!"

A wave of compliance overtook me while I scowled at my mother, her brow furrowed in concentration. Despite the extensive power I had at my disposal, it always seemed to me that Mom's ability to make people feel *exactly* the way she wanted them to feel was *probably* the most dangerous magical ability on the planet. I was protected against anything that could come at me —except my mother.

"Blood ties us," she said after scanning my face. "You're my daughter, I always have a way in. Remember *that*."

Gunther's head peaked in the back as I sat down at the table. His eyes focused on me, and then my mother. With a nod to himself, he pulled his head back and closed the screen door.

"Traitor!" I called after him.

"Drink," Mom said. She set a glass of sweet tea down in front of me. "You look as frazzled as you used to during finals week, Charlotte."

"I *feel* that frazzled," I sighed and guzzled down the cold drink.

"Tabitha looked positively stricken when she came in here," Mom said. "Are the two of you not getting along again?"

"Her dad's sleeping with Melissa Hayden," I told her in between gulps.

"No! But she's so young, and he's so...Well, I *would* say old, but I expect he's the same age as I am. He *is* so *married*!"

"Yep," I nodded. "I wish I had time to catch you up on everything that's been going on, but the long and the short of it is, Tabitha's father is a big old jerk, and she's having trouble handling it."

"And you?"

"My father isn't a big old jerk, so I'm handling things better, I guess," I joked with her wearily. Mom clucked her tongue at me, and I smiled.

"We're doing the best we can. Everything's just complicated right now."

"How so?"

Darn compliance energy.

I peeked out the back screen door at the group assembled there waiting for me. I could see Tabitha on the swing next to Bob. She was speaking softly to him. Gunther and Kyle conversed in muffled tones on the opposite side of the porch. Turning back to Mom, I whacked the table.

"Fine. In a nutshell? Sarah Stevens kidnapped Samson with Raven Goodfellow's help, but Raven Goodfellow is actually the love child of Samantha Goodfellow and Darius Stevens."

"No!" Mom looked shocked by my revelation.

"Yes," I nodded and held out the glass to Mom so she could refill it. "We're sure Raven doesn't know. Well, we *think* he doesn't know. Tabitha had no idea until last night that he was her brother."

"That poor girl!" Mom said as she passed a refilled glass back to me. "She found *that* out and *then* that her father was having a relationship with one of her friends all in the *same* night?"

I nodded. "We have no idea if it's related to what's going on, but it sure could be."

"If Sarah Stevens knows, clearly that young man could also be in danger." That hadn't occurred to me, but to be fair, consideration for Raven Goodfellow's safety in any capacity hadn't occurred to me.

"Eh, I met him. I'm not worried about him too much, honestly," I told her, shrugging. "He was kind of creepy. And he kidnapped Tabitha. Not a great guy, so who cares, really?"

"Charlotte Astley, I'm surprised at you," my mother's eyes tightened. "Since when did you lose your empathy for people? You always give people the benefit of the doubt."

"I don't doubt he stole my cat and drugged his mother. Besides, it's easy to give people the benefit of the doubt when I can read their minds. I couldn't read him well, and what I could read was just nasty."

"He drugged his own mother?" she asked, horrified.

"Well, Sarah did. Drugged his mom. But he had to have known, right?"

"Couldn't you see it in his mind whether he did?" Mom asked.

I looked back at my mother's steadfast gaze and then dropped my eyes. "I…um…I've been having some trouble with that lately," I told her as I shifted restlessly.

"That's to be expected with the lawgiver powers," Mom said in a matter-of-fact tone as she gestured toward the ring. It glittered on my hand as if it heard her. "It could also partly be because of Samson being gone so long. Anyway, unless you know that he knows *for sure*, I wouldn't assume *anything*, Charlotte. Especially if your telepathy skills are shaky."

In the blink of an eye, the edgy tension returned, and I ceased feeling obliged to listen to my mother.

"That's unfair, you know." I propelled myself away from the table.

"Mothers use what they have in their arsenal, Charlotte," she called after me as I headed for the door. "Someday, you'll find out for yourself."

Sure.

If we lived through this.

Gunther got us back to the Makepeace Circus with what seemed like an effortless snap of his fingers. Ambom, one of the circus's guardian gargoyles, rambled up to us with his eyes glowing

that distinctive ruby red. It simultaneously scared
the heck out of me and made me want to make
jewelry out of it.

"Lady ringmaster! You come with man
ringmaster!" the slobbering beast greeted me
excitedly. With a precipitous halt, he stopped and
positioned his blade toward Bob. "You are
warrior from 'nother circus! You attacking?"

"Brother!" Bob beamed as he laid down a
weapon I didn't even realize he had in front of
the living gray stone beast. "I humbly request
approval to enter the territory you look after,"
Bob said. He sank to one knee and bowed his
head. "I come not to conquer but to break bread
with you!"

"If you break bread, I kill you," the gargoyle
snarled as his brother gargoyle, Irum, hurried
over to us. "You no break nothing here at circus.
You break things? I break *you*."

"Ambom, what Bob said was a phrase that
means he wishes to dine with you as friends," I
told the gargoyle standing in a defensive posture.
"You know, break bread? As in rip pieces off and
eat them together?"

"My mouth bigger than his." Ambom scraped
his hard head with a long, dangerous-looking
claw. His face creased in consternation, the lines

cracking loudly like heated rock. "Don't know how we eat one piece of anything *together*. Ambom would eat the face of Bob. Wouldn't mean to," Ambom said apologetically to Bob and shrugged. "Just would."

I sighed.

"Ambom, we'll work out dinner arrangements later. For now, know that everyone here is a friend," Gunther said. Tabitha looked surprised. Ambom nodded and stood up from his threatening attack stance. Somehow, the added height made the creature even more terrifying. "We're going to my father's cabin."

"Your cabin," Ambom corrected.

"Yes, ah, you're correct, of course," Gunther nodded sadly. "We'll be in my cabin if you need us."

"Wow, is this *your* circus?" Tabitha asked. Her head swung around inspecting the more extensive, fancier, and much more modern amusement park.

"It is," Gunther nodded proudly.

"It's *a lot* nicer than Charlotte's," Tabitha murmured.

"Our circuses were constructed to project different auras," Gunther said with an awkward cough. "My father thought it was much more important for us to integrate seamlessly into the contemporary world. Charlotte's circus is a throwback to the more classic, big-tent circuses of old."

"I like this a *lot* better," she said. We ascended the steps of Gunther's log cabin home.

"Thanks," I told her wryly.

"Not a problem," she countered with a bow when Gunther opened the front door.

With a twist of his hand and a pop, my boyfriend produced a huge chalkboard at one end of the living room, immediately in front of the assembled couches. Kyle made a beeline for a container of chalk that manifested right next to the board and snatched a stick from the pile.

He began writing.

"Why did you want to come here instead of going to my place?" I asked Gunther—as if we had just left a movie and picked one person's apartment over another.

"As soon as we walk onto the Magical Midway, Ms. Elkins will come at us. Not to mention the fact that Jeannie's passed away, Aidan's ill, and the fact that we haven't found

Samson will panic your people," Gunther said, pulling me into a back hallway. "I think we should check on all of that, but I'm not sure we have time for you to stop and deal with all of it."

"Cauldron?" I pointed to the room ahead.

Gunther nodded. "Just remember that the cauldron isn't exactly private. Don't say anything you wouldn't want the Council to overhear."

"Are you telling me the cauldron lines are tapped?"

"No...I...You can't consume the liquid in the cauldron," Gunther told me, confusion clear across his elegant face. "The liquid is for—"

"Never mind." I leaned forward and gave him a kiss. "That whole 'came from two different worlds so we don't even use vocabulary the same way' thing happens less and less. Tapped means that someone is listening to your phone call or something without you knowing. Someone taps into the communication. Get it?"

Recognition spread across his face, and he nodded.

The mists rose, and soon Fiona was staring angrily at me. "Where the heck have you been?" she shouted, leaning forward and wagging her finger at me so hard that it leaped out of the fog fully formed on this side. "Your uncle is inconsolable, your past reader is comatose on your couch half-dead, Fortuna's painting images of fire and water like she's in a bloody trance—"

"Slow down, slow down!" I shouted.

"Slow down? We've been worried sick for you and scared half to death for us, I'll have you know! Sunset and sunrise passed and nothing! Nothing! Wait a minute," Fiona leaned forward, her eyes narrowing dangerously. "Are you at the Makepeace Circus? You *better not* be at Gunther's place while we're here losing our collective paranormal minds with worry—"

I sliced my hand through the mist and muted the conversation. Fiona continued to diligently read me the riot act and Gunther exhaled slowly. Her hands whizzed in and out of the fog.

I turned and stared accusingly at Gunther.

"Sorry?" he smiled sheepishly. "Honestly, love, I really thought it would be quieter here. Wayland does a good job of keeping the place in order without me, so I knew we wouldn't be disturbed."

"Can I borrow him?" I asked as I side-eyed my enraged kelpie friend.

"Not if I have to trade him for her." Gunther nodded toward Fiona. "Your circus always seems…ah, a little higher strung than mine."

"You know, Ms. Elkins came from *your*

circus," I pointed out. "Things were calm before..."

"Not *that* calm," he smiled.

"Wait...she came from *your* circus." I jerked my head up, startled. If I was the center of the universe destined to yadda yadda yadda, why hadn't Elkins been at the Magical Midway?

"Yes, she did," he answered, confused.

"If *I'm* the Thirteenth Witch, why was she at *your* circus?" I asked him. "For *years*?"

"I don't understand what you mean."

"I don't yet, either," I told him, hanging up on Fiona. "But I will figure this out if it kills me."

Gunther stared at me.

"Okay, poor choice of words."

CHAPTER 15

"He's asleep," I said to Kyle, and then related what Fiona had told me. "She was furious we hadn't been back—but on the plus side, she seemed more interested in screaming at me about it than saying what they needed. That tells me things are fine over there. More or less."

Kyle gave me a look of concern.

"Look, Aidan's not *dead*," I snapped, and plunked down on the couch in front of the two chalkboards, now filled with information. "What more am I expected to do from here?"

Tabitha gasped, unable to hide her shock at my flippant dismissal of Aidan's current state. Gunther stared at me, his face grim. I rolled my eyes.

"Look, I'm not trying to be a jerk about this, Kyle—and you two can stop looking at me like I just kicked a puppy," I said, growing uncomfortably embarrassed under the accusing stares of my friends. "I just can't give you any more information than that."

"I didn't *ask* for any more than that," Kyle responded quietly.

"Your *face* did," I grumbled.

"Look, everyone is getting discouraged about how long this is taking." Gunther placed a hand on my shoulder from his spot behind the couch. "Maybe we should go through this information as quickly as we can. After, we can stop by the Magical Midway and check on the situation there."

"Do we have to?" I asked reluctantly. More glares. "Okay, okay, sorry. That's a good idea."

"Right," Kyle exhaled. "Well, here's all the suspects," he said as he pointed to the board.

"Not all," I murmured again as I noticed Tabitha's name had been omitted from the *possibly guilty* board. I glanced over at her to find that she was glaring straight at me, her jaw nearly down to her chest. "What? I'm still not *absolutely* sure that you're *not* involved in this somehow. The apple not falling far from the tree and all—"

"I have had it!" Tabitha shouted so emphatically the ceramics rattled on the sofa table behind us. "You know what, Charlotte? You have turned into the most imperious, insensitive, uncaring—"

"*I* have? *I'm* not the one hanging out with dope dealers and hoodlums," I said, jumping off the couch to face her. "I realize it must be *super* hard having crappy parents and a bigoted ex-fiancé and all, but people's lives *depend* on me, you know! I can't get too bound up in any *one* thing or person—"

"So you somehow have more right to be a *jerk* or something because you're so *important*? Besides, how could I forget you're *super important*? You won't let anyone, not for a hot second!"

"Ladies, I think—" Gunther began.

"You stay out of this!" Tabitha told him fiercely before spinning back to me. "I *get* the cat is critical to you, and I *get* that it's the center of the magic that keeps your two circuses protected. Believe me, I understand all of this mythological *as the parchment turns* garbage—"

"Garbage! This is our world, Tabitha!"

"And this is mine!" she screeched at me as she pointed her finger to the ground. I opened my mouth to argue that she was really aiming at a magic floor in a magic circus in a magic in-between world, but she continued without taking a breath. "It wasn't bad enough my best friend leaves. Not bad enough that my father is having affair after affair. It's not bad enough my mother started hanging out with the town mobster night after night, it's not bad enough—"

My blood ran cold.

"Wait a minute, back up," I waved at her. "What did you say?"

Tabitha paused, straightened up, and squinted. "Which insult did you want me to repeat?"

"No, no, no—your Mom was hanging out with Michael Hayden?" I asked her, walking closer.

"Well, at his restaurant, yeah," Tabitha said with a small shiver. "Her drinking this past year got a lot worse than it used to be, and she started hanging out at his bar until all hours. I felt like a complete idiot if you want to know the truth," she said, looking down. "Melissa and I introduced them, kind of. Mom took us out to dinner there, and Melissa suggested—"

"Her mother *hung out* with the man that was being *targeted* by her husband," I said to Gunther.

"So…so does that mean Sarah and Darius are

working *together* to get Maggie's power?" Gunther asked in a bewildered tone. "That's what it *seems* like. Right? What else could it mean?"

Kyle frowned as he thought about it.

"My mother and father working *together*?" Tabitha laughed wistfully. "There's no way. They can barely stay in the same room with each other without a riot breaking out."

We were missing something.

I stood on Gunther's considerably sized porch alone, observing the Makepeace Circus go about its day as if nothing was happening. There was no noticeable sign that anything in his circus was amiss just by looking at it—although we were *all* hiding.

Gunther was right.

My circus was higher strung than his.

Well, they didn't know about their potential link to Samson, or that Samson might look after them, too. As far as they were all concerned, this was a relief mission because the Magical Midway was in trouble.

Again.

"I didn't mean it," Tabitha whispered from the door. I shifted and looked at my old friend, her eyes bright even though her face seemed etched into a perpetual frown. "About their circus being better than yours. I didn't mean it."

"Yes, you did," I smiled sadly and shifted away from her.

"Can we talk?"

Without turning to look at her, I nodded.

We stayed next to one another, overlooking the small houses that the Makepeace citizens called their home. Children played in makeshift front yards, and the cheerful shrieks of babies punctuated the silence that had fallen between us.

"This isn't us," Tabitha began, but I cut her off.

"Yes, it *is*," I told her, turning. "You and I are not the same anymore. We were fools to think we were."

"No, you're right," she said with a sigh. "We're not the same. That doesn't mean that we're *enemies*, though, Charlotte. You've got enough of them with this Witches' Council thing. I don't know why you're working so hard to turn me into one, too," Tabitha paused. "Or why I'm trying to turn you into one. I'm sorry. This has just been hard for me."

I didn't reply.

"I can't do anything other than promise you I'm not *willingly* a part of this. I can't guarantee you I'm not a *part* of it *at all*—obviously, my kidnapping took place just to lure you back here, and I *get* that. And," she turned to me, her eyes glassy with unshed tears. "I'm sorry about that. Truly, I am. As happy as I was to see you again, I wish that you'd stayed away."

"How could I?" I asked her. "I *knew* I could find you. I didn't know that the police could."

"You know what happens when people are forced to care about everything, Charlotte?"

I raised my eyebrow.

"Eventually, they care about nothing. Because it all becomes too much. It's starting to happen to you, right now. I can see it."

I stared, thinking quietly. I wanted to argue with her, but I couldn't. Humans could only take so much before they just shut down. Maybe super-powered witches were no different.

"You may be going through precisely what happened to the Witches' Council, how it all went bad. You know? Even with more power than anyone else, no one can resolve everything."

"And when no one else has any power because

one person is hoarding it, they can't fix anything for themselves," I muttered. Tabitha nodded.

I had known that when I took over the Magical Midway. I set up a leadership council, a court system. I knew exactly what needed to be done to help people empower themselves.

Then, somehow, I had taken it all back as the prophecy slowly convinced me I had to have it.

"It's that stupid prophecy," I breathed staring up at the Ferris wheel. "Ever since Ethel Elkins showed up, she's simultaneously made me feel completely controlled *and* like the entire world rests on one choice that I have to make. I don't even know what that choice *is*."

"Maybe it's not *one* choice," she shrugged. "Maybe it's a bunch of small decisions."

"Maybe."

We stood side by side a little longer watching an acrobat flip down the dirt road. He settled with a splat and gave a wave, then flipped the rest of the way toward a tiny house.

"I don't want to fight with you anymore," Tabitha said. "But I feel like for us to not fight you have to trust that I'm on your side." Tabitha paused. "Do you? Can you?"

I turned to my old friend and searched her

eyes. Minutes passed as I examined her, sensed her, remembered her.

Finally, I nodded.

"You will help us even if your parents are behind all this?" I asked her as we went toward the door to head back inside.

"If my parents are behind this, I'm sure your Witches' Council dragged them into whatever horrible things they were encouraged to do," Tabitha said as she held open the door for me. "My parents *aren't* great people. They're ethically challenged, and narcissistic as *all* get out, but they're *not* lunatics. I have to believe they wouldn't really hurt anybody."

"I hope you can still believe that when this is all over," I told her as I went inside.

"Me, too," she whispered as she followed, so low I could barely hear it.

Kyle and Gunther turned to inspect us cautiously when we returned. Bob jumped up, looked me up and down and—once I reassured him I was unharmed—ran over to Tabitha.

"We're fine," I said and held my hand up. "Look, I'm sorry to everyone—I feel like I'm adopting Samson's temperament or something because I miss that dumb cat so much."

"Yeah, don't do that," Gunther warned.

"Where's your kitten, by the way?" I asked as I looked around the house for Delilah. "I feel like I haven't seen her in ages."

"She's hanging out with the circus cats," Gunther said.

"You have more than one cat?" I asked. He nodded. "Like, *real* cats? Not were-cats?"

"Galenite witches," he said.

"Gala-*what* now?"

"Witches punished by the Witches' Council," Gunther said as Tabitha's mouth fell. "We don't get imprisoned in the traditional sense of the word like other paranormals. We're turned into cats as punishment and forced to serve the Witches' Council as familiars. Those that manage to escape their servitude have few places to go. My father gave them sanctuary, so many show up here once they learn there is a place they can hide."

"Why don't we have any?"

Gunther shrugged. "Samson, maybe? Honestly, I don't know. I can't talk to them."

"So how do you know what they are?"

"They're marked with a Theban G on their fur in silver."

"Theban?" Kyle asked.

"It's an occult alphabet," Gunther explained. "We've hypothesized the G might be part of the spell that keeps the soul bound within the cat. No one knows for sure, though. It's not like we're taught the spell in school."

"You know, your world gets creepier and creepier the more I hear about it," Tabitha said, shaking her head.

"Is Delilah a Galenite witch?"

"No, she was freeborn," Gunther told me.

"What about Samson?" Kyle asked. Gunther shrugged. "You don't know?"

"No one truly knows what the guardian is," Gunther said. "He's obviously not just a cat or just a familiar. And he's not marked," Gunther pointed out. "So I wouldn't think so."

"So, question," I said as I held my finger up. "Yes?"

"How would you know whether a Galenite witch cat thing was someone running *from* the Witches' Council or someone working *for* the Witches' Council?"

"Well, because...I mean, clearly, if someone showed up here, and they were...The other cats would know," Gunther said, nodding to himself. "The other Galenites wouldn't accept the newcomer. I'm sure of it. And we do *have* the Witches' Council protection."

"Against the council. Are you sure it would work against the cats? Or that the other cats would say something?" I asked skeptically.

"Would they have the same tie that you guys have to your cats?" Tabitha asked. "Being able to know where they are and all that?" Gunther looked pained as he shrugged again.

"Charlotte couldn't find Samson without Devana," Bob pointed out.

"That's because of where he was, though," I told him.

"Look, the cats? They're not all that smart. They're called Galenite witches because they use Galena to enforce the witches' confinement in the cat bodies," Gunther explained.

"Wait, wait, wait a minute—what do you mean confinement *in* the cat bodies?" Tabitha cocked her head. "I thought they just turned the witch into a cat. Are you trying to tell me that there's, like, a soul shoved in a *real* cat?"

"Well...yes," Gunther answered slowly. "Bound by Galena."

"What's Galena? Is that a goddess?" Tabitha asked.

"A rock."

"It's the natural form of lead," I told her.

"So you *poison* a cat with *lead* and *shove a soul in it?*" Tabitha asked, outraged. "That's horrifying!"

"Well, *I* don't do that!" Gunther huffed, offended.

CHAPTER 16

"Oh..." I exhaled.

"My gosh..." Tabitha whispered.

"They're everywhere. Absolutely everywhere," Kyle announced as if we couldn't see the furry mass of cats for ourselves.

Then he sneezed.

We entered an enormous, hanger-sized storage building and the cacophony of mewling, meowing, whining cats and kittens was almost deafening. Black cats, white cats, striped cats, calico cats. Long-haired and short-haired and no-haired cats lay among pyramids of hay bales, folded up towels and stretched out blankets.

"That one doesn't have the same mark," Tabitha pointed to a small black kitten that ran in front of us. The young cat was being followed by a massive white cat with a silver letter that looked kind of like a U on its backside.

"If two Galenite cats mate, they'd have a litter of regular kittens," Gunther explained. "So, many of these cats are Galenite cats, but many of them are just regular cats that were born here. Most of the older cats, the ones born here, leave eventually, so the young ones that you see are 'typical' cats. The older cats? Mostly Galenites that showed up here for refuge."

A streak of black flew toward Gunther's head, and Bob shouted for him to look out. Without flinching, Gunther threw out his hands and snatched Delilah from midair. Cradling the small cat, he kissed her on the nose. She returned his affection with a rough lick and a meow.

"She's gotten bigger," I said and reached out to pet her. The young cat hissed fiercely at me, and I snatched my hand back instinctively.

"Um...sorry about that," Gunther smiled sheepishly. "Dee's been a bit unhappy with my absence."

Delilah hissed again.

"You call her Dee now?"

"In cat growth stage, she's a teenager," Gunther explained. She smacked his chin with her paw. "She felt Delilah was too sugary and not tough enough now that she was growing into a mighty hunter."

She hissed again, clearly still upset.

"Boss, can't you read any of them?" Bob asked as he walked back carrying a pure white Galenite cat with a shining silver marking. "I mean, you're a telepath or an empath or something, right? There are witches stuck in there. Can't you, like, peek in their heads and find out what they know?"

I took a deep breath and opened my mind, hoping that my telepathy or empathy (or whatever it was I was *supposed* to be able to do) would work. As I closed my eyes, a waterfall of images hit me from every angle as hundreds of witch-cats' thoughts invaded my awareness. I heaved an unsteady breath as my eyes flew open.

"All I can sense is the animals' thoughts. That's not something I can normally do," I told Bob as I reached out to Gunther for support. My head was dizzy as the images faded from my mind. I felt a little like I had vertigo. "If there are witches' in any of these cats, I can't discern them alone. Their thoughts are all wrapped up with the cats."

"They're really all twisted up together. At least from what I understand," Gunther said as Delilah scrambled to the top of his head. "They know who is who, but…so, I can talk to Dee, and she can talk to the cat, and the cat can talk to the witch, but that's the only communication pathway we have. And it's an awkward one."

"You put two cats in between in the game of telephone," I said thoughtfully, gazing at the hundreds of apathetic felines. Most of them didn't even bother to look at us, and the few that did stared coldly with narrow, apprehensive eyes. "That's two chances for the conversation to break down."

"Yeah, I mean, we just don't really bother anymore."

"Well, they seem happy here," Tabitha kneeled down and scratched the belly of the white cat with a silver marking. "The cats, anyway. I can't believe it thrills the people trapped in them to be there."

"The cats get a longer lifespan," Gunther shrugged. Delilah launched off his head and ran after the white cat she had been playing with. "There's always hope. We've never been able to figure out how to separate them, though. At least not safely."

"My father," I said as I looked out across the

vast room. "We can bring my father here to talk
to them. And they can talk to him as well."

Tabitha looked slightly bemused. "He can talk
to cats, too?"

"Any animals," I told her. Her eyes widened
slightly as she stood up. "Well, *any* living thing.
Trees, bushes, grass. If it's alive, Dad can have a
discussion with it."

Kyle looked at me with interest.

"Let's head over to the Magical Midway,"
Gunther said. "Maybe after this is all over we can
go see your dad. Do you think he would help us?"

"Of course," I shrugged. "Why wouldn't he?"

～

"It's about time you showed back up!" Fiona
shouted when the five of us approached my yurt.
"Don't have the cat, I see," she said, searching each
one of us up and down. "Gallivanting around the
old home town, are we? Did the old friend take
you on a trip down memory lane in the slowest
vehicle she could find? Are we—"

"How's Aidan?" I asked, ignoring her rapid-fire
series of verbal attacks disguised as queries that
she never paused long enough for me to answer.

"You *remember* him, do you?" she asked me with anger rippling across her face. "He's on *your* couch sleeping like a babe from a fairy tale, wouldn't you know. No, you *wouldn't* know, *would* you? Because we've *scarcely heard from ya!*"

"Are you *finished?*" I rubbed my fingers wearily into my eyeballs. It seemed like Tabitha and Fiona were two sides to a coin. As soon as I stopped fighting with one of them, the other stepped up to take her place.

"You deserve more," Fiona snapped. She leaned her back wearily against one of the poles that appeared to hold my yurt erect. "You left me here with your poor uncle who's going mad trying to find Jeannie's lamp so we can lay her to rest—"

"Her lamp?" I asked in confusion.

"We bury djinns with their lamps," Fiona explained as I approached her, her voice emptied of its resentment but still saturated with the same weariness I was feeling. "*In* their lamps, really. They're used like a coffin. It's tradition, and your uncle is beside himself that he can't find it—"

"He can't *find* it, or it's *missing?*" I asked deliberately.

Fiona blinked. "Well, we thought—"

"What are you thinking?" Gunther asked me as he joined us.

"We've been racking our brain trying to figure out how they would steal our energy, right?" I asked Gunther. "What *human* magic could they possibly get a hold of that could steal ringmaster power? None that we could think of, right?"

"Unless they had a bound genie," Gunther whispered, his face turning white. "A bound genie *could* grant the transfer as a wish. That book Raven got. *The Capture and Turning of Monsters* was the name of it."

"The genie and the lamp thing? Three wishes and all that. That's *for real*?" Tabitha asked, shocked. Gunther nodded.

"It's the slavery of a paranormal person, but yes, if a human found the lamp and knew the magic words? Absolutely. It would bind Jeannie to that human until her obligation to him or her was complete," Gunther said.

"But we found her…glitter dust stuff," Tabitha pointed out.

"Sparkle ash," I said distractedly.

"We found sparkle ash," Bob acknowledged. "We did not, however, turn it back into her body to see if it was *really* Jeannie."

"Or if it's even sparkle ash at all."

"You think someone stole her, too, and left a pile of glitter to make us think she was dead?" Gunther asked me.

"Sarah said on that phone call we overheard they had the *beings* they needed—not 'the cat.' 'Beings' is *plural*. But how would someone *know* to do that?" I asked as I glanced out over the carnival. "Someone would have to know *where* she hid her lamp, *how* much sparkle ash a body produced—"

"And what else?" Tabitha asked, her eyes bleak and her look troubled.

"What else what?" Bob asked her.

"What else would they have to *know* to have been able to do this? If they were human, I mean," Tabitha asked. "There has to be more information than that. The magic words for the lamp, where the lamp was, and what sparkle ash looked like. What else?"

"Nothing, really," Gunther said after reflecting.

"Are you *sure*?"

"Gunther went to school for this stuff, so he's probably right," I told Tabitha, crossing my arms. "Why?"

"Because I got access to an old book at the university when I was looking for you. I told them I was doing research for a thesis. Handwritten over a hundred and fifty years ago. Supposedly about your circus," Tabitha paused, looking fearful. "Well, it had *all* those things in there," she said quietly, her eyes pleading with me not to accuse her of this.

The five of us stood together in silence. Then Kyle spoke.

"Was anyone else with you?" he asked softly.

She nodded.

"Who?"

Our eyes met.

"Melissa Hayden."

"Uncle Phil?" I asked gently as I entered his home alone.

The yurt was dark, and it smelled of agony and tears. Candles glowed from mounds of wax. My uncle must have been in this room, staring at the sparkling mass of ash since we left. The air was heavy and thick.

"Charlotte," he answered roughly, his usually clear voice hard as if he had smoked a thousand cigarettes. As the death of his love had settled over him, Fiona told me the grief had sought to pull him down into the gloom. From the looks of it and the feel of him, it had succeeded. I'd never seen my uncle in this state before. "Have you found Samson?"

"No, Uncle Phil," I told him and wrapped an arm around his hunched back. "We know where he is, though. He's safe for now." Angry, alone, and miserable, probably. But not hurt. Not yet.

"You should be out looking for him," he admonished me in a whispered, gravely voice. "You're a ringmaster, Charlotte. Checking in on your dead uncle keeping watch on a pile of sparkle ash should be the *least* of your concerns."

"I know, Uncle Phil, but…" I stumbled, desperate not to give my uncle false hope, but determined to find out if our hypothesis was right. "I heard that you can't find Jeanie's lamp," I began. "Maybe I can help you find it."

"That would be wonderful, Charlotte. I've looked everywhere," my uncle said as one hand reached out and lay flat against the sparkly possible remains of the djinn. "I hate to see her here out in the open like this. It's not natural. But I can't even find the safe she kept it in."

"Well, tell me what I'm looking for, and I'll scan for it. Jeannie kept her lamp in a safe?" I asked casually. This corroborated what Tabitha had read at the university. The curious book outlined that Jeannie kept the lamp in a small metal safe.

"Of course!" he responded with a hint of his old spark. "That's not something you would just put out to hold flowers or pour tea, Charlotte. It's powerful!"

"I know, I know, I just mean—"

"It was in a small safe in her kitchen!"

I reflected back to Jeannie's shack and flipped through my recollections of it. I recalled seeing an antique metal safe with a modern padlock in the back corner. And also on top of the fridge. And on the oven once.

"Uncle Phil, could someone pick up the safe? Or was it magically protected?"

"*No one* could pick up *that* safe! There are an *incredible* number of magical protections surrounding the thing!"

"Oh, good—"

"Well, unless they were human," Uncle Phil interrupted my relief. "They technically made the lamp *for* humans and not for her, after all. No way to keep *humans* from opening up the safe if they wanted to."

I exhaled.

"What? What's that sigh?"

"Why would she keep it out there in the open like that?"

"So those that needed her would find it," he answered, his hand reaching out again to lightly pat the glitter mound. "She adored being a genie. She didn't mind the occasional binding, not if she could benefit someone that needed her. It was why she was created, after all."

"What if someone enslaved her?"

"Oh, she had ways of talking to them," Uncle Phil smiled wistfully. "If she didn't want to be there, she had the means of ensuring they would get clear of her as hastily as *she* wanted to be gone."

I stood next to him silently as Uncle Phil sank back into the silent depth of his grief. I had found out all I could. I had to change the heap of sparkle ash back into Jeannie—if the ash was, in fact, my uncle's companion.

I believed it wasn't, but I had to be positive.

"Uncle Phil, why don't you go take a shower?" I asked him and leaned against his bulky body struggling to help him up. "You must have been here since we took off."

"I have, and I will be here until her interment," Uncle Phil told me decisively.

"I can sit with her," I told him, shoving harder.

"Quit poking me, young lady!" Uncle Phil barked as he thrust back.

"Sorry, Uncle Phil," I said, and I mumbled for him to be deaf, dumb, and blind. In the flutter of an eye, an inky blackness surrounded him, and he stilled. One hand still reached toward the pile of sparkles, and I gently tugged his hand away.

Squeezing my eyes shut, magic surged as I muttered the spell that reversed the festive sparkle ash combustion that was a Magical Midway death.

With a deep breath, I opened my eyes gradually, my muscles tense, to find—

—just a heap of glitter.

This wasn't Jeannie. Someone had faked us out.

And now I knew who at least *one* of those people might be.

CHAPTER 17

As I returned to my yurt after seeing Uncle Phil, I found Devana leaning over Aidan. She was staring keenly into his face as he snored loudly on the couch. Gunther looked over at me, and I gave him the thumbs up.

"It wasn't her," I reported and then gestured to Devana. "Welcome back. Any change?" I asked.

"Oh, good, you're back." The huntress rose up and twisted around. "I have news. Jeannie is not—"

"Dead. We know," I interrupted.

"They have kidnapped her with—"

"Samson. We know that, too." Devana's face fell at my quick reply. "My wild guess is that she's being held in the grotto along with my cat, and they're hoping we will show up there. Yes?"

Devana's teeth gritted in irritation, her eyes squinting at me.

"Sorry," I shrugged. "We were busy, too, you know. Am I right?"

"Yes," Devana frowned. "And she's bonded to…" Devana held out her palm toward me and waited for me to finish her sentence. When I didn't answer, she inclined her head and said with a tinge of snark, "No? Have I turned up *something* you have not? For all my work, have I accomplished at least one important thing? That would be *gratifying*, I must admit."

"Melissa Hayden?" I guessed. I had been suspicious of her from the moment I found out she was seeing Tabitha's father. Devana shook her head no.

"My mother?" Tabitha chimed in only to get a negative headshake. "Okay, then my father?"

"That's two guesses," I told her.

"And two wrong guesses," Devana answered. "Bob?"

"The Witches' Council?" he asked with a smirk.

"That's probably three guesses, but no, and I should point out they are not human," Devana pointed out to the lares. "The Council could not have bound the genie to them. Fiona?"

"I've been stuck here," she griped. "I don't know any of these people." She swung her head to look at Kyle. "What about you, centaur? You were a detective, were you not? Who do you think took the genie?"

We all turned to look at Kyle. He shuffled uneasily from foot to foot as he tried not to look at the huntress witch he so loathed. Images flipped through his head, and as he settled on one suspect leaning against a desk, I gasped.

"It was *right there!*" I exclaimed. Kyle met my eyes and nodded.

"We didn't notice," he said. "We weren't looking for it."

"What are the two of you talking about?" Fiona asked us archly. "Don't leave us all here in suspense."

"Michael Hayden," Kyle and I said together.

Tabitha doubled over with laughter as every other face registered shock.

"What's so funny?"

"You realize that we've overlooked the *one* guy we knew from the get-go was a murdering, sociopathic criminal for sure," Tabitha said as she wiped tears away. "The *one* guy that we knew was the head of a mob, who has the town in his pocket, who organized the overthrow of his boss while *serving as the victim's right hand.*"

When she put it like that, it *was* a little embarrassing.

"I have to admit, that guy's *good,*" Tabitha said as her laughter trailed off.

"I followed Melissa and Darius from the magic shop," Devana explained when we all sat down to compare what intelligence we had accumulated so far. "At first, it seemed that they just didn't want to be in our company anymore," she said as she raised an eyebrow. "Once they arrived at the Stevens household, it was clear that Melissa was far more involved than we had suspected."

"How so?" Tabitha asked as she eyed Devana suspiciously.

"One sign was the fact that Melissa Hayden hit your father in the head with a baseball bat as soon as they were behind the closed door," Devana told Tabitha. "Then she tied Darius up with rope and—"

"Oh my gosh," Tabitha gasped, unable to hide her surprise or worry. "Is my father okay?"

"He has quite a large bump on his head, but she did not manage to crack his skull," Devana reassured her.

"Well, I guess Dad really *isn't* involved in all this," Tabitha said, her voice reverberating with astonishment. "Either that or Melissa's, like, really mad at him for the cheating thing. I have to admit, I didn't see that coming."

"The baseball bat?" Bob asked. "Neither did your father!"

Tabitha looked at him incredulously.

"Well, if he had, he would have ducked," Bob pointed out.

"I understand what you meant, Bob."

"Right, sorry," Bob said with a mix of devotion and regret. "At least Devana was able to help him."

"I didn't say I *helped* him," Devana corrected Bob. "I said his skull wasn't fractured, so he was in no urgent danger. I had to remain unseen."

"Where is Darius Stevens now?" I asked her, trying to refocus the group on the issue at hand. "Did Melissa take him, too, or leave him at the house?"

"She loaded him in a trunk and took him with her," Devana answered. "Unwillingly, I might add."

"That girl could barely walk without a crutch!" Tabitha looked at her. "My father is twice her size, and at least twice her weight. Did he crawl into the trunk on his own?"

"He was obviously unconscious, and she easily carried him."

"That makes little sense," Gunther said as he sat down.

"It makes *some* if they've *already* spent some wishes," Bob pointed out. "They only need one to take your power. They have two others to bring about whatever they want in support of that."

"I know what they did with one wish," Devana said as she pointed to Aidan. "They needed to lure you all to the cavern for what they wish to do. Aidan would have been able to unmask their plans as soon as he met one of them."

"The other must've healed her fully," Bob nodded.

"And given her super strength," Tabitha mumbled.

"I know this is kind of silly, but when I saw *Aladdin*," I said slowly—a little embarrassed to bring up a genie lamp theory that I got from a Disney movie. "Iago stole the lamp before Aladdin wished his three wishes. Jafar still got to make wishes even though Aladdin wasn't *done*. Do they *work* like that?"

"If that's the case, then they've got *three* wishes for Melissa," Tabitha said. "*Three* for Michael, *three* for my mom, and *three* for Raven. That's an overall total of—"

"*Twelve* wishes," I exhaled.

"That's *a lot* of wishes," Devana said.

"Maybe even another three for my dad," Tabitha said. "That would be fifteen. Fifteen chances to take the Magical Midway power. As well as do whatever else they wanted."

"Let's stick with *twelve*," I told her. "I feel like your dad will not be amenable to helping them out with wishes after being tied up and hit in the head with a baseball bat."

"No, you're probably right."

We all sat around the coffee table stunned at the enormity of their arsenal against us. Occasionally, someone shifted in their chair, but the revelation was staggering. They had multiple chances to be right. We only had *one* chance to defeat them.

"So how do we fight them?" Gunther asked after a long period of silence.

"We don't have to get the *cat*," I said, wincing. "What we have to get is the *lamp*."

"We can't get the lamp," Devana said. "I tried. There is powerful *magical* protection around it. I couldn't get near it. No paranormal can get near it, much less make a wish on it while Jeannie is bound to a human."

"Right." Gunther's gaze shifted over to Tabitha. "No *paranormal* can." Tabitha stared back at him. "She's *not* paranormal. She's human."

"No, no way." I stood up and waved my hands. "There's *no way*! It's too risky!"

"And you going *isn't*?" she asked in exasperation. "You could lose everything!"

"We *all* could," Samantha Goodfellow said from the doorway.

I stood up, shocked. "*How* did you get here?" I asked in a strangling gasp .Panic rose within me. "We're in a place you shouldn't be able to reach! Are you *part of this*? Are you some type of paranormal now?"

Gunther touched my arm lightly to calm me, but it didn't work. If she could get here, the rest of them couldn't be that far—

"Just human, dear," the heavyset priestess answered as she stepped in. Behind her entered her chorus, and my eyes narrowed. "I realize they are not, however," she said with a smile.

Our entire party (sans the snoring Aidan)

surged up and confronted the three women, who transformed into Mina, Mabel and Mercy World. The evil witch trio faced us with sober looks etched into each of their faces. I lifted my hand to get rid of them.

"Hold, Ringmaster!" Mercy boomed without raising her hands in defense or offense. The other two with her stared passively. "Before you dismiss us and put our entire world in peril, hear what we have to say. If you still wish to banish us when you have heard, so be it."

Gunther stared at Mina, the witch that had taken over his body, with scarcely contained rage. Devana, too, stared her down with a contempt so visceral I could practically taste it.

"We could not come here if Maggie had not allowed it," Mercy pushed. "You *know* this. If Eiggam and Maggie could lay aside their dispute to focus on this menace, *surely* we can."

No one had ever *told* me that, but I knew deep within myself that she was right. This was our safe space, a place animated by Maggie's energy. They shouldn't even be able to *detect* us here, much less come to it with ease.

The door to Ethel Elkins' room opened, and the old norn emerged for the first time since we returned. All of us rotated to watch her shuffle toward an armchair, glare at Kyle to step aside from his place in front of it, and settle in at the head of the lounge area.

"Let them speak," she proclaimed imperiously as if it was her decision.

The four women walked toward the seating area.

"Hold up there, folks. *I* didn't say you could speak," I told them. The high priestess suppressed a smile as Ms. Elkins face grew angry. The three Council witches frowned, but their progress ceased.

This could be a trick, I thought to Gunther. He looked at me and shrugged his shoulders almost imperceptibly. *This is about you, too. Your circus, too. What do we do?*

The women stared at me.

I glared back.

It's up to you, Gunther said.

*No, it's up to **us**,* I thought, and I held out my hand to him. He looked down at it, startled, and Devana stepped away from me to make a place for him. *We do this **together**, right?*

His face was so solemn that I almost laughed. But I didn't laugh. Everything about this was significant, somehow, and I think we both felt it. He stared at my hand, obviously torn about whether he should take it, whether he should step into the place that had been made for him.

A grin spread across his face as he strode forward and seized my hand.

"Wait!" Ethel Elkins shouted as she struggled to lurch up out of the chair.

They told me later the discharge of energy from our hands touching was so extraordinary that there wasn't a living being in either circus that didn't lose consciousness for *at least* a split second.

CHAPTER 18

"WELL, *NOW* YOU'VE DONE IT," MS. ELKINS grumbled as she awakened, glaring at me. Behind her, Mina climbed up off the floor and dusted herself off, looking enraged.

"What *was* that?" I asked, bending my elbow to examine my hand clasped in Gunther's. "We've held hands many times, and nothing like that has *ever* happened before. Do you know what that was?"

Gunther shook his head. *I don't, but I feel like we should perhaps wait to discuss it,* he thought to me. *With the Witches' Council here…Well, no need to give them any more information than they already have.*

You're probably right.

"We'll listen to what you have to say," Gunther told them. "But only if you restrict yourself to the truth."

Everyone in the room looked dazed, shocked, or curious. Gunther ignored the psychic explosion that had taken place and refocused on the Witches' Council as if nothing had happened.

"*Bind* ourselves to the truth?" Mina scoffed, speaking for the first time. "What, oblige *ourselves* to be subject to *your* lawgiver powers even though you *cannot* compel us? Are you *mad*? Do you take us for fools?"

"Not *subject* yourself to them," I shook my head. "Well, not all of them. Just confine yourself for a defined period to only speak the truth. All three of you. You won't have to answer a question if you don't want to," I said. "But I don't want to waste my time with this if you're just going to lie to us. We can accomplish more faster if we don't have to play games."

"We don't know if you're involved in this. You being here?" Tabitha said (quite ironically) as she lifted an accusing finger and pointed at Mina. "This could all be part of your plot. This *whole thing* could be *your* plot. Showing up here and claiming to care about the outcome could be nothing more than a fake-out."

Mina leaned forward and stared at Tabitha imperiously, her eyes narrowing. "Are you *human?*" she asked Tabitha haughtily, sweeping her gaze over my friend.

"You don't know?" Tabitha asked with a small smile. "Not much of a witch, are you?"

Mina's eyes flashed with anger. I stifled a laugh.

"Fine, if it will move this situation forward," Mercy said. Mina turned and stared at her sharply. "What? It is a fair request. We *have* been trying to destroy them. It is the fastest way to establish our intentions, Mina."

"Mina doesn't wish her intentions established, I imagine," Devana said with a crooked smile. Mina swung her head back and shot her venomous look at Devana.

"This has nothing to do with us," Mina told her.

"It has everything to do with us, *sister,*" Devana shot back, raising her chin defiantly.

"You're on the wrong side of history," Mina countered.

"I'd ask history, but he's been felled by a wish," Devana said as she pointed to the snoring Aidan still asleep on the couch. "Convenient for you that someone has silenced him, isn't it?"

"Okay, enough, ladies," I thundered. I stepped into the space that divided the two women. Turning to face Mina, I restated our condition one more time. "Bind yourself to the truth or leave this place. Those are your two options."

Letting loose a string of salty curses under her breath, Mina whipped around and placed her hand out, palm down. Mabel and Mercy placed their palms gently atop Mina's hand as Mina began muttering.

"Out loud, please," I called. "So we can hear you."

Mina shot me an angry side-eye glance. I shrugged.

"Let only truth fall from our lips," Mina said, and the two women repeated the words. "Let there be no dishonest…blips," she said, and they echoed. "Until the moon doth rise tomorrow, allow our party help avoid this sorrow." Mina dropped her hand with a flourish. "Satisfied?"

"Um…I guess?" I looked at Gunther. "I mean, that was a pretty non-specific spell. And not that great. Blips?"

"It doesn't have to be great. It just has to bind them."

"*I* can test Mina." Devana moved toward the head of the Witches' Council.

"Devana!" Ethel Elkins snapped, but the huntress ignored her and kept moving toward the woman she felt betrayed her entire clan.

"Answer me *this*, Mina," Devana said, creeping forward like a cat stalking a mouse. Only the mouse was not inattentive in this case—Mina was tense, her eyes tracking Devana's every movement. "When you left the village to hunt Eiggam for his power, did you give thought to the infant daughter that you left behind? Or did you *rejoice* to be free of the burden of the helpless child?"

"Clearly not so helpless," Mina shot back.

Mina stared, her eyes angry. I looked back and forth between the two women seeing something that I had not seen before—even though it had been *right* in front of me.

A resemblance.

"*Tell* me, sister," Devana purred. It was a menacing sound.

"Devana, I forbid this," Ms. Elkins voice cracked again. I glanced over at the old woman. She looked worried.

"I am *not* your sister, and you don't know the whole truth," Mina whispered.

"You are not *anything*, and you know *nothing*," Devana spat back at her.

"Devana, it's enough, little wolf," Ms. Elkins said in a gentle tone, pushing herself from the chair. "Don't do this to yourself. Come with me. Come."

"Wait a minute," I told Ms. Elkins as she reached out to pull Devana back. "You were there when the huntress witch caused the rift between Eiggam and Maggie," I told Ms. Elkins. "And you're fighting them because it's your responsibility to heal this schism for your people," I said as I pointed at Devana. She nodded sharply once, never taking her eyes from Mina.

"Wow, this is convoluted," Tabitha murmured.

"But why you?" I asked Devana. She didn't answer. I inquired again, and she remained mum. "Well?" I asked Mina.

I knew.

Honestly, I couldn't tell you how I knew.

But I knew.

"Mina, are you Devana's mother?" Gunther gasped in my mind. The rest of the group might have gasped, too, if the tension hadn't sucked all the oxygen right out of the yurt.

"I don't have to answer you," Mina whispered, her eyes filling with resentful tears.

"Yes, that abandoning, treacherous witch is my *mother*," Devana spat out angrily.

A silence fell as if someone banged a gong. Mina looked shaken and on the verge of weeping. Devana's expression continued to crackle with resentment and fury.

"Well," Tabitha said finally as we all stared at Mina. "I didn't see *that* coming."

Being a ringmaster was often like shepherding a beloved but scheming elementary school class—if that class was filled with arrogant sociopaths possessing superpowers. They all *meant* well, but their decisions had such destructive potential. The fact that I never seemed to know the full story about anything constantly hampered my ability to help.

"Can you work with her?" I asked Devana after I pulled her into a corner.

"I thought you would ask me why I chose not to tell you," Devana said as we huddled together.

"I want to know that, I do, and don't think I'm not super-annoyed that there's yet another thing I didn't know about until you shoved it into my face at a *critical* time," I told her. "But honestly, it happens so often I'm getting used to it. And right now, Jeannie and Samson are depending on us."

"I understand," Devana nodded.

"For the purposes of getting them back and saving our collective rears, *can* you work with her? For *one* night?"

"They have raised me to do what I must." She stood up straight, re-cloaking herself in the aura of steadfast control that had defined her until now.

"Raised by Ethel Elkins?" I guessed. Devana nodded.

"My clan ostracized me, abandoned to the snowy hills as the offspring of a traitor," she said, wincing as though speaking the words was painful. "Ms. Elkins found me and took me in. Raised me as her own."

"From an infant?"

Devana nodded once.

"And you don't call her mother?"

Devana nodded again. "She is *not* my mother. I have no mother."

Obviously, she did, but as I glanced at Mina World, I realized going through life as an orphan might be preferable to claiming that horrible woman as a mother.

"I will do what I must do, Charlotte," Devana assured me, bowing her head. "I promise you. You can count on me." She glanced hatefully for a moment toward the woman who betrayed her in her first moments of life. "I keep *my* commitments."

"Okay, let's hear it," I told Mina, Mabel, and Mercy. "Why are you here, and what do you propose?"

"Are we not going to deal with the revelations of—" Mabel began, but I cut her off.

"No."

"But we—"

"Now that we realize they have access to genie wishes, Samson and Jeannie both are in graver danger than we thought," I said, cutting her off a second time. "The *humans* can't kill Samson, but I suspect Jeannie *can*. We've been operating on the premise that Samson was safe for the most part, if uncomfortable. That's no longer the case."

"They cannot kill the cat until you arrive," Mina said. She leaned against the wall of the yurt. "The two of you must be in physical proximity to one another for the energy to be transferred. Wiping out one of you would give it to the other. Destroying both of you separately would dissipate that energy into the world so that a little of it goes to every living thing on the planet."

"Done a lot of thinking about this, have we?" I asked her with a head tilt.

"You *have* made it harder for them, however." Mina waved her hand toward Gunther. "Now they must get the three of you near one another before Jeannie can wrench the power from you."

"Why the three of us?" Gunther asked.

"Because you just joined the circuses," Mina said with an exasperated eye roll. She held up her hands and linked her two forefingers together like a chain. "Your power is now *his*. His power is now *yours*. Romantic, really," she added with a slight gag.

Gunther and I stared at one another.

"What did you *think* would happen when you gave up your power to a man?" Mina asked me. "It's not an action you can just take and then reverse when you change your mind. Decisions have *consequences* in our world."

"For everyone but you, it seems," Devana murmured.

"I didn't *give up* my power to a man," I snapped. "If what you're saying is true, we both just became *twice* as powerful as we were. Sounds like the joke's on you."

"You made sure what I was saying was true," Mina snapped back.

"We're getting side-tracked with all the independent woman wand waving," Tabitha said. "Let's get back to how we will get Jeannie and Samson back."

"We take them," Mina shrugged. "We are the most powerful witches in the paranormal world. Surely we can work together and rescue a *cat*."

"And what about Jeannie?" Devana asked.

"Djinns are illegal," Mina said with another shrug. "You can see *why* they are illegal considering *none* of this would have happened if you didn't have one."

"Jeannie's a person, not a *pet*," I sputtered.

"Pet, person, whatever," Mina shrugged. "Illegal. She should not exist."

"You can't make *people* illegal," Tabitha told her.

"Oh, but I can," Mina said ominously. "And I did. This is not your world, human. Do not put *your* values on *me*. You are unimportant to our paranormal world."

"Maybe in *your* eyes, but apparently *your* world has to be saved by a human," Tabitha told her. "So, I'm clearly not *that* unimportant. And with you in charge? I don't even know if I *want* to rescue you people."

"Look, Tabitha—"

"Yeah, yeah, I know, I know," she raised her hand to stop me. "It's not just your folks in danger but my parents, too. They're horrible people, but they're still my parents. I owe it to them to try, even if I'm just saving them from their own stupidity."

Devana and Mina stared across the room at one another silently as the group began to formulate the plan that would save us all.

CHAPTER 19

DOORS BANGED IN THE DARKNESS AS WE PILED OUT of cars so packed full of people it astonished me they didn't explode. The cicadas' rhythmic droning was the only sound that broke the silence. We were back at the peaceful, isolated country road that led to the grotto of power.

"This way," Tabitha said and strode straight toward the dirt path we had climbed once before. Bob closely followed her. I stepped in the middle of the cortege with the Witches' Council silently behind me. Kyle marked the tail of our solemn procession, bringing up the rear.

Devana and Samantha Goodfellow approached from the opposite direction with Gunther. We had determined that our ability to talk telepathically would be more useful if we were in divided groups—and if things went south? It would be harder to get us in physical proximity to one another to steal the power.

It didn't take us long to arrive back at the hole that widened to expose a hidden chamber holding the now-churning magical pool. As we peered in through the broken dome, I could see Samson in a cage.

Water gushed over the drenched cat, whose jail hung on a rock beneath the waterfall. Jeannie sat just to the right of him in front of the cascading flow, her lamp on a pedestal beside her. Both of them appeared safe *and* defiant, pugnacious expressions on their faces despite the circumstances.

I returned my eyes to poor Samson. He sat quietly under the continuous deluge of cascading liquid. My heart broke for him, guilt coursing through me as I saw with my own eyes his suffering. Suffering I had caused him by not coming sooner.

"There's no one near them," I whispered.

"Yes, there is, look," Tabitha pointed, and I stretched my neck. A silhouette moved against the chamber wall just a few feet from Samson and Jeannie. Then another shadow. There were people in the passageway leading to the grotto down below. How many, though, I couldn't tell.

"They know we will go for the lamp," I whispered. "Why else would they have it out in the open like that? It has to be a trap."

"Shhh, quiet—someone's coming out of that hall!" Tabitha pointed and we crouched even further down.

"I assumed they would be here by now!" Raven Goodfellow shouted. He raced out of the hallway toward the waterfall. "What am *I* expected to do, *teleport* them here?"

"You're *such* a moron," Sarah Stevens snapped, following him.

"*You* have powers!" Raven snapped back, and pivoted to face Tabitha's mother. "If you'd just *use your last wish* and turn over the stupid lamp to me, we could have this all over and done with!"

"*No* one will persuade me to give up my last wish," Sarah warned him. She sauntered over to it and patted its gleaming top. Glaring at Jeannie, she continued. "That woman is my get out of jail free card in case this all goes south."

"You mean *our* get out of jail free card," Raven corrected.

"Sure," she agreed distractedly, after she took a

swig from a flask pulled from her pocket. "*Our* card. It's *our* card."

Tabitha gulped, her eyes anguished, as she watched her mom walk around the waterfall.

We're here, Gunther thought to me. *But so is Michael Hayden. He hasn't seen us, but we just saw him go in the back entrance.*

"Showtime," I sighed to the collected group. Mina nodded.

I stood up and stared down at my friend's mother.

~

"Mrs. Stevens," I barked.

Her head snapped up, a broad smile spreading across her face. "Charlotte!" she shouted with excitement, her voice reverberating against the walls of the cave. Waving her hand toward the waterfall, she gleefully announced she had found my cat.

"You *kidnapped* my cat," I told her, Tabitha still out of sight near my feet. "You took my cat. All for what? To get my power so you could punish your husband?"

"And his *little girlfriend*," she hissed. "Don't

forget about that little science experiment of a tart."

"You mean Michael Hayden's sister, Melissa?" I demanded, and the color drained from her face. Sarah's jaw dropped open so far that if she had been standing a little closer to the waterfall, the woman just might have drowned. "You *didn't* realize that was his sister, did you? If you had known the man you got entangled with was the *brother* of the girl sleeping with your husband, would you have *still* followed his plan?"

"I...I don't know *what* you're talking about," she stammered and reached into her pocket again for her flask. Raven appeared transfixed on me, his upturned face bewildered. "I don't know Michael Hayden. This was all *my* plan!"

"You've spent half of this caper drugged and drunk," I responded. "Granted, you got away with more than I would have guessed you were capable of, but I still think you're capable of far less than all this on your own."

"I am capable!" she screeched. "I am good! I—"

A slow, loud, clap echoed from the hallway behind her, and she stopped howling at me to turn toward it. As I peered into the darkness, Michael Hayden emerged from the shadows.

"You *are* sharper than I gave you credit for," Hayden called up to me. The criminal was smartly attired as if he were going to a country club and not hiking through the woods. He looked composed.

"You're *less* honest than I gave you credit for," I called down. I crossed my arms. "Once I realized Jeannie was still alive, I knew it had to be you."

"Well, I'm a criminal, so there was always a good chance it was me," he quipped. "I'm surprised you gave me any credit for honesty at all. What gave me away?"

"The lamps in your office," I told him. "That, and you knew who Jeannie was. That she 'died.' I didn't realize until later that you couldn't have known unless you were the one that had her. You didn't have contact with anyone that would have told you."

"I didn't expect you to show up that day," he shrugged. "It threw me off my game, I suppose."

"What happened to your line about owing me for keeping your sister from getting shot? Or owing Gunther for fixing her? That whole 'I have a code' thing?"

"Well, I wasn't planning on *murdering* you."

Michael pushed Sarah out of the way and pointed toward Samson. "Or the cat, for that matter. No one needs to die here."

"That's what owing someone means to you? You don't kill them?"

"I said I owed *Gunther* a favor," Hayden responded, shrugging again. "And I don't see Gunther here to make a request. Do you?"

"Who *are* you?" Raven glanced around in confusion. His head swung back and forth as he studied Sarah, Michael, and me with visible unease. "How did you even get *in* here? *You're* not a member of the coven."

"*You're* not a very smart young man, are you?" Hayden asked him as he proceeded to move toward Samson and Jeannie. "I suppose the cat's out of the bag now. Or," he laughed, pointing. "The cat's in the cage."

"The cat is—" Raven started, but Michael Hayden cut him off.

"I *arranged* all this, Mr. Goodfellow. I exploited all of your secrets to get you *all* to do what I wished. So I could get what I want." He paused and then pointed at me, towering above him. "Her power. And once I had it, to hoard enough henbane that no witch could ever challenge me again."

"But…no…That can't be right. You're *not* a witch," Raven thundered accusingly. Turning to Sarah, he confronted her. "How could you do all this for a muggle!"

"A 'muggle'?" Mina snorted behind me disdainfully.

"I served you as my high priestess!" Raven screamed shrilly. Sarah cowered back from his fury. "You said this was about the Goddess! About the coven! You lied to me!"

"Oh, shut up, bast—"

"*Why* did you *lie to me*?" he went on, contempt dancing in flushed red waves across his pale face as he walked menacingly toward her. Even as Sarah pulled away from him, fury flashed in her eyes.

"Because you're my husband's illegitimate spawn, you contemptible little—"

"Mother!" Tabitha's voice cut through the cavern like a gleaming silver blade.She shot to her feet and glared down into the cave. Sarah's wild eyes met Tabitha's furious glare. "It's not Raven's fault that Dad had a thing with his mother. He had nothing to do with it. Leave *my brother* alone."

"Brother…" Raven whispered, tumbling to the ground, his face white.

"Your *brother*? Tabitha! Tabitha, I…" Sarah's

voice broke, and she appeared caught between resentment and desolation. With a whimper, she began to sob. "I never wanted you to know."

"Well, I *know*," Tabitha confessed. "He's family, whether you like it or not. Leave him alone."

"Oh, Tabitha," Sarah wept, her shoulders slumping. "I wish your father and I could go back the way we used to be. Back before the drinking, before the anger, before the cheating. We were *so happy* once, idealistic hippies that would change the world for the better. I wish we could be that way again…"

She lurched toward a boulder, any self-possession and pride she had disintegrating like the cave ceiling.

"Done!" Jeannie chimed out, her voice ringing in the grotto.

The metamorphosis was as extreme as it was fast. Sarah Stevens's eyes cleared, her tears drying. Tense lines on her features softened as if she underwent a face-lift. Pushing herself off the rock, she stood tall, her back erect and took a deep breath.

Then her face registered horror and shock.

"Oh, my goddess, my husband!" Sarah screamed, her voice clear and high as she raced to the water's edge. "He's in the flooded cavern, we have to help him!"

"We've got this," Mina whispered behind me. As the three women joined hands, Sarah Stevens and Raven Goodfellow disappeared just as her body belly-flopped into the churning pool.

"What did you do?" Tabitha snapped at them.

"She's in the cave with her husband," Mina said.

"So's he. The gothic boy. They're both safe," Mabel told her. "For now, at least."

"We absolutely don't want any *more* humans near that lamp," Mercy explained with satisfaction as she jerked her chin in the direction of the grotto.

"If you could do *that*, why not just put *him* in the submerged cave?" Tabitha asked them loudly as her arm angrily extended toward Michael Hayden.

"Oh," Mercy sighed, the smugness fading from her expression. "Yes, that would have been a good idea, too."

"Oh, my gosh, sometimes you people astonish me," Tabitha quipped as she whacked her hand to her forehead.

"We can't," Mina said, her finger shaking as she pointed it toward Hayden. He looked up, smiling. "Something is impeding me." Mercy and Mabel rested their hands on Mina's shoulders, and the witch's finger glowed even more brilliantly.

"Did you *really* think I hadn't used one of my wishes to ensure I was not subject to your witch magic?" Hayden asked with a lopsided smirk. "I'm not an idiot."

"Neither am I," Melissa said as she stomped out from the shadows to stand beside her brother. "So, now that you know you can't do *anything* to us at all, how about we get on with this?"

Tabitha and I stood with the Witches' Council high atop the grotto, looking down at the villains below.

"Has Samson tried to talk with you at all?" Tabitha asked.

"There's something about that water that seems to block telepathic communication," I shook my head no. "I can't get a sense of Samson even though he's right there."

"But I could do it when I was in the ritual room. Reach out to you, I mean."

"You weren't *in* the water," I pointed out. "He is, technically."

"Plan B, then." Mina studied Tabitha. Tabitha shuddered. "Unless you have *another* proposal. But if we cannot magically influence him, we can only transform our team. And *you're* the token human here."

"Fine," Tabitha shrugged, her shoulders drooping. Bob looked concerned. "Just get it over with."

Mina, Mercy, and Mabel stacked their palms on one another's and murmured a spell in a language I didn't know. As they did, I detailed to Gunther what we were doing and watched Tabitha flicker out of sight.

"Oomph," I grumbled as my friend, now invisible, hopped on my back. I staggered as she threw off my center of gravity. "Jeez, gained some weight, have we?"

"You have superpowers, you'll be fine," Tabitha muttered in my ear. "*Don't* drop me. I *don't* have superpowers, and if I slam into these rocks on the way down, it's gonna hurt."

"I've got you," I mumbled as I began my walk down the trail into the grotto alone.

Well, alone as far as Michael and Melissa Hayden knew, anyway.

CHAPTER 20

AS I PICKED MY WAY PAST THE BRUSH AND INTO THE rock-enclosed path, Tabitha balanced on my back, I tried to determine who had wishes left.

Sarah said she had only one—and then promptly made it when Tabitha's appearance rattled her. If she had already wished *two* wishes, she was *probably* responsible for Aidan's comatose state and Samson's inability to communicate with me as he was being kidnapped.

I had *no* reason to think they gave Darius any wishes. With Tabitha's father locked up in the underground cavern? That took *him* out of the mix for now.

Michael and Melissa Hayden turned to stare at me when I entered through the small tunnel behind them. The pathway I followed had wound fully around the grotto through the rock walls before it rejoined the rear exit. Samson was only ten feet to my right, Jeannie just five feet beyond him.

"I wish that—"

"Just hold on a second," I said while I tried to shift Tabitha's weight without giving away that I carried my friend on my back. "Before we do this whole thing, I have to know—have you been playing me from the very beginning?"

"From the *very* beginning?" Michael asked and then tilted his head. "Not from—"

"I wasn't talking to *you*," I told him and pointed to his sister. "I was talking to Melissa."

"Me?" she asked in surprise.

"Yes, you," I nodded. I glanced down at the slick rock. If I placed Tabitha down here, they'd see her footprints in the sheets of liquid. I had to get her closer to the lamp. My arms were aching regardless of my super-powered strength. Despite my faith in the plan—which, honestly, was a *fantastic* plan—I was tense.

"What do you mean, *playing* you?" Melissa asked suspiciously.

"You didn't seem to know what your brother was when we first met," I told her. I peered at

Samson and tried to walk casually toward him. Michael and Melissa seemed more focused on my words than my stiff gait as I crept closer to the ledge. "And you seemed like a *nice* girl. Honest. Caring."

"*Crippled*," she added and placed her hands on her hips.

"But Gunther helped your body to heal." I now stood next to Samson's cage. "Is *this* how you pay people back that try to help you?"

"*Help* me?" She took three long strides up to me and jabbed her finger in my chest. I exhaled loudly as I felt Tabitha's arms and legs release me quickly. From what I could tell, the two women had just barely avoided a collision between Tabitha's arms and Melissa's hand. The spell ensured no one could *see* Tabitha, but she still had mass that could be felt.

"Yes, help you!" I said, stepping closer to her in hopes that I could block her view of any footprints Tabitha may have left on the damp rocks.

"*Help* me?" she asked again, incredulous. "He could have healed me with a snap of his fingers! Instead, I had to claw my way upright! All the while, the doctors are sticking needles in me and poking around trying to figure out *what on earth is happening!* How could you people think that was helpful! It was horrible!"

"Is *that* why you did this?" I asked her. Her face was so close to my own I could feel her breath on my lower lip. "You're angry we didn't heal you all at once?"

"My *brother* healed me," she said, "without lies and without delay." She went on to explain that he used his first wish to not only heal her entirely but to make her as indestructible as he could. "I'm strong," she said, her eyes glittering with hatred. "And it's none of your business *why* I did this."

I stepped back from Melissa and closer to Samson and Jeannie. Michael had used at least two wishes.

That meant he had one left.

"I didn't lie to you because I wanted to, Melissa. I lied to you because our worlds are *supposed* to remain separate, so things like this *don't* happen."

"Things like *what*? People getting back what they never should have lost in the first place?" she demanded, her eyes flashing tears of frustration. "*You* don't deserve it."

"And you do?"

Melissa turned away from me and picked her

way back over to Michael. "My brother and I both do. We're not selfish. Like you."

The lamp clanked against the pedestal. I froze.

"What was that?" Michael asked. He leaned forward and examined the brass-colored lamp carefully and then looked back at me. "What are you doing to the lamp?"

"I can't do *anything* to the lamp," I told him. I held up my hands and wiggled my fingers. "Paranormal, remember? And I have no doubt you know that—otherwise you never would have let me near it. Only humans can get near *that* lamp." I reached out, and a flash of light zapped me. "See?"

Jeannie snorted. I glared at her. She smiled at me and gave me a thumbs up. I rolled my eyes.

"Michael, just *take* her powers!" Melissa demanded.

Michael waved her quiet. He examined me and then Jeannie, whose face held a smile so full you could count her pearly whites from ten feet away.

"I am so sorry that what Gunther did has caused you such pain, Melissa," I told the wish-granted woman—who looked angrier than her brother. I couldn't understand how I had pegged Melissa Hayden so very, very wrong—I knew her brother was a dangerous psychopath pretty much from the get-go.

She *hadn't* been, though.

Love, we can worry about this after we take care of Samson, Gunther thought to me. *Maybe it's time to bring this to an end.*

I knew Gunther was right, but the raw pain and anger in Melissa's eyes held me.

There was something here I wasn't seeing.

"I wish to be a ringmaster, Genie," Michael Hayden told Jeannie. "My final wish is to take power from that woman and her cat. Grant me my final wish so I can pass you to my sister."

"Yeah, so *about* that," Jeannie said as she stood up and walked over to me, "since Charlotte's gotten married, we'd need Gunther here. You'd have to take *his* power *and* her power, and for that, they both have to be here. I'm not totally omnipotent."

"I got *what* now?" I stared at Jeannie.

"*What* are you talking about? Of course you are," Hayden snapped.

"Sure, I'm *close.* I'll admit that. But there are things even I can't do easily. And regardless of *that* little fact," Jeannie continued and put her arm around me, "*you* don't have control of the lamp anymore. I'm bonded to another human now."

That statement was all our hidden comrades needed to come pouring into the humid grotto. They entered by foot, they manifested via teleportation, and Bob just jumped through the hole in the roof.

I grabbed the cage and yanked it out of its watery prison. Placing it on a boulder, I pried open the door and pulled out a coughing, hacking black cat. The Witches' Council pinned the Hayden siblings to the cavern wall with a sparkly pink mist.

Samson! Samson! Are you all right? Can you hear me?

I can hear you, woman! You're shouting in my brain! Samson screeched back so loud that I winced.

I am so sorry, I told him as I squeezed him tightly. Gunther raced across the boulders toward us, relief written across his face. *You tried to tell me what was happening, and I ignored you.*

Is he all right? Gunther asked telepathically as he joined us.

Of course I'm all right, Samson said.

Gunther pulled back and blinked.

"I heard that," my boyfriend said out loud.

"Heard what?" I asked him slowly. Even though I knew.

Of course you heard that, you moron, Samson told him with a hiss. *I can't believe the two of you got married without me. It's ridiculous. And during this crisis.* The cat settled down on a boulder in front of me and began to clean his fur.

We didn't get married!

You did.

"Why are you saying that?" Gunther asked him softly.

Maybe the two of you newlyweds should pay attention to what's going on here, Samson retorted. *You still have problems. Unless you don't care if the humans live or die. In which case we can talk about this all now if you like.*

Gunther and I looked up to find Devana standing in front of Samantha Goodfellow, balls of menacing-looking lightning floating in her palms as she faced down the Witches' Council.

CHAPTER 21

"Whoa, whoa, Devana, man, calm down!" I dropped Samson back onto the stone and raced over to the angry huntress witch. It looked like a magic attack chain with the three Council witches' palms out against the mafia siblings, Devana's palms up against the three of *them*, and Bob sweeping his arms wide as he looked for Tabitha.

What is she so upset about? Samson asked.

Apparently, Mina is Devana's mother.

That explains a lot, Samson thought back. *Actually, that makes no sense. Are you sure?*

I am, I told him. *A lot's happened since you've been under that waterfall.*

Well, had you paid attention when I tried to call to you—

Not now.

I think that's what you said when they were kidnapping me, too, if I'm not mistaken, Samson responded haughtily. *How did saving my comment for later work out for you again?*

I turned around and stared at the cat as he carefully groomed the water from his fur. *Okay, you have my attention,* I told him as I stared at him. He continued his leisurely tongue bath without looking up. *Well?*

I was just going to give you a lot of grief for neglecting me before and allowing me to get abducted, he said. The black cat stopped his grooming and peeked up at me, eyes sparkling. Then he sneezed. With an ear flick, Samson tilted his head. *That can probably wait.*

"Aargh!" I shouted and rotated around to survey the scene before me. Bob was flailing haphazardly, Devana was sparking menacingly, and the Witches' Council witches were pink-misting casually. Melissa and Michael looked back from their immobilized places on the rock wall.

"Don't even *think* about killing those humans, Mother," Devana shouted as she blazed the fireball in her hand. "I can see that savage look in your eyes. This isn't up to you."

"*Everything* is up to me, Devana," Mina told her quietly without tearing her eyes from the humans. "That's the point of being the head of the Witches' Council." Her eyes narrowed as her fingers flexed. Mabel stood next to her, looking confident, but Mercy's gaze nervously jumped from Mina to me. "There have never been two humans that were as significant a menace as these two. No mortals that *begged* for death as noisily."

"I didn't join forces with you to thwart their plan just so you could kill them, Mina," I protested as I pushed Bob out of the way and spun him to face the podium. "The lamp, Bob!" I told him as I pointed toward Jeannie's lamp. "She's over by the lamp!" Bob nodded and shot in that direction.

"Who…is…?" Michael gasped roughly, the pressure holding him flat against the wall, making it hard for him to breathe.

"Tabitha. The Witches' Council made her invisible," I told him. "She came down with me. She's got Jeannie's lamp. Speaking of Tabitha," I said as I turned to Mercy and hitched my thumb in the lamp's direction. "Could you all make her visible again?"

Mercy snapped her finger in Bob's general direction, and Tabitha reappeared behind the pedestal, her fist wrapped around the lamp tightly.

"Thank you," I responded. Mercy nodded.

"How…could…you…have…helped…them?" Melissa gasped at Tabitha.

"Could you let *off* them?" I urged, glaring at Mina and pointing to the cave wall.

"Nothing they have to say concerns me. They should not leave this grotto," she countered, her fingers flaring out and more pink, sparkly smoke spewed from the center of her palm. "*I should deal* with all these people so that this risk is put down once and for all."

"All of *what* people?" I asked suspiciously.

"Any human with an awareness of our world," Mina responded with a condescending frown.

"What do you want to do, wipe out this entire town? Move on from that and attack new-age retreats?"

"No matter what you may think of me, Astley, you can see with your own eyes the complications generated by our worlds intermingling. None of this would have taken place if we had kept the wisdom hidden."

"*Wisdom?* First of all, *that's* rich. Second of all,

here's the thing," Tabitha said as she strolled over to me and glanced at Mina pointedly. "*I* have the lamp," she declared as she dangled the small genie lamp from her index finger. "It would suggest to me *I'm* the one in control here. Not *any* of you. So, rein it in, your highness. I have three whole wishes, and I'm about to fling 'em."

Mina looked pointedly at Tabitha's hand— now wrapped firmly around the brass ornament. The witch tried not to reveal any concern, but her deep-set eyes dilated just enough to indicate her fear.

"So, how about we let them down off the wall, huh?" Tabitha was joined by Bob, his face set in a glower, as the two of them challenged Mina as one. "I mean," Tabitha continued, "I'd *like* a diamond necklace or something cool, sure. But watching *you* go up like a Roman Candle *could* be fun, too."

"That would be *terrible*," Bob gasped to Tabitha. "A slow, torturous death depending on the type of tallow."

"Oooh, *that's* wicked," Tabitha grinned and looked expectantly at Mina. "Wanna melt like the witch in the *Wizard of Oz*? Only *really* slowly, and while your hair's on fire?"

I was pretty sure Tabitha was joking.

Pretty sure.

Mina, however, was *not* sure.

"I do *nothing* because you ask me," Mina snapped, dropping her hand to her side. "They're human, it's not like they could disturb any of us now that you have the lamp."

The two captives tumbled to the ground with a thump.

"Right," Melissa gasped as she clambered to her feet. "Because it's not like we got you all here in the first place or anything. Jeez, you people are so cocky," she spat. She brushed herself off. "But you! I can't believe you sided with them after all that's happened!"

"Maybe if you trusted me, Mellie, we could have got what you wanted without people getting hurt," Tabitha said wistfully.

"Wait a minute. You *knew* about this?" I choked and whirled to stare at my friend. "Have you really been part of this all along?" Bob looked torn and perplexed again as he tiptoed away from Tabitha toward me.

"Don't get your panties in a bunch, Charlotte," Tabitha rolled her eyes and slung the lamp at me to wave my shock away. "And you, Roman?" she pointed to Bob. "Get back here. I didn't know Mellie was part of it way back when. But I expect I know why she did it."

"Shut up, Tabitha," Melissa stammered, her eyes shifting toward her brother.

"She did it to help me!" Michael told Tabitha, but Tabitha shook her head. "I think I know my sister better than you do."

"She didn't. She did it because she wanted to use a wish to get her parents back."

"I…I…" Melissa gasped and paled, her hands shaking. "I just wanted things the way they used to be," she whispered as she crumpled into a ball against the cave. "I didn't think anyone would get hurt. I didn't think Michael would—"

"Would what?" he asked her coldly.

The young woman dropped her head and whimpered softly.

Tabitha explained Melissa's emotional journey to us as the girl sobbed. It was a journey inspired by the healing of her legs and the revelation that magic was real.

Once Melissa realized the material they were discovering as they searched for me could lead her to a genie lamp, the girl became obsessed with gaining the magic that would undo the accident that had taken so much from her family.

"I didn't understand just how obsessed she had become," Tabitha admitted. "If I had, I would have tried to help her through it more."

"That crash ruined *everything*!" Melissa cried as Tabitha wrapped her arm around the weeping girl. "It turned Michael into an awful man. Everyone assumed I didn't realize what he was, but I *knew*. I knew the day he killed his boss and took over. I knew what he did to Tiffany. I knew Michael was a criminal."

"That's how you knew he would help you come up with a plan to get the lamp," I speculated. "You knew he was power-hungry enough to do it." She nodded.

"I didn't know he would manipulate so many people, though," she said , looking at Michael. He stood over her, patiently taking in everything he was learning with no reaction. "I told him I didn't want him to hurt anyone or murder anyone or anything."

"I haven't," he maintained.

"I don't know that no one's been *hurt*," I pointed out as Samson jumped on my shoulder. "Samantha Goodfellow was drugged repeatedly,

Raven and his mother's relationship is probably damaged. Samson—"

"You, cop," Michael called to Kyle as he gazed down into the water. "Was anyone *technically* hurt in all this from a legal perspective?"

Kyle stepped back over and tilted his head. "You drugged people against their will—"

"Me, *individually*? I did not." He crisscrossed his arms.

"You are fantastic at making sure your hands are clean, aren't you?" I asked him.

"It's a gift," Michael told me ruthlessly.

"Could you even do that?" Tabitha asked Jeannie. "Bring people back from the dead?"

"Sort of?" she said with a thoughtful expression. "They don't come back exactly the same. It would be far easier to change these two into who they would have been had their parents not been killed, or had the accident not happened. Raising the dead? That's a complicated business."

"You did it with Charlotte's Uncle Phil," Tabitha pointed out.

"Not really," Jeannie disagreed. "Phil is still dead. He's just a ghost with a body."

"Why are we bothering with all this?" Mina shoved her way into our circle. Tabitha narrowed her eyes and lifted the lamp slowly in Mina's direction. The witch raised her palms. "Don't *wave* that thing at me. I just asked a question."

"We're bothering because I have three wishes to make, and I'm trying to figure out how to use them," Tabitha told her. She gestured to me. "Can you go get my parents and Raven? The way you got me when I was down there?"

"I'll do it," Gunther said as he touched my shoulder. He turned, dove into the tranquil water, and melted into its depths.

I raised my eyebrow at Tabitha, and she winked.

Samantha Goodfellow wrapped her son in her arms once Gunther returned the three to the surface. I stared in shock as Sarah Stevens slipped over the rocks in a rush to embrace both of them. Her apologies to Samantha for how she treated the woman echoed off the walls.

Darius, looking deflated, hung back as he stared at the ground.

Sarah turned to him and held out her hand. "Darius, come," she encouraged, and he hesitantly went over, tears rolling down his face, to embrace the two mothers of his children. He whispered apologies to them, and to Raven, for his actions.

Melissa hid her face in her hands, blushing.

"Did you actually encourage your sister to *sleep* with Tabitha's father just to further this plot?" I asked Michael. He shrugged.

"It was the fastest way to get an in with him," Michael told me, looking back at the two families. "Women are his weakness."

"You are *seriously* gross," I told him.

"It almost worked, didn't it?" he sighed down at his weeping sister. "I thought Melissa had finally grown up a bit. I suppose I was mistaken."

What a pig.

"So, now that everyone's up here," Tabitha called loudly over the enormous cave. "I'd like to make my wishes."

"We didn't talk about that," I began.

"Nope, we didn't," Tabitha agreed. "But they are *my* wishes, aren't they?" she asked as she turned to Jeanie. Jeannie nodded. "Before I make them, though, can I ask you some questions?"

I chewed my lower lip nervously.

Jeannie stared at my friend as if she were about to say no when Samson jumped on Jeannie's shoulder and patted her head with his paw. She reached up and scratched my cat's chin, turning back to examine Tabitha again with curious eyes. After a few moments, she nodded yes. Samson purred.

You want to tell me what this is about?

Nope, the cat responded.

"Are my parents' decent people now?" Tabitha asked as she pointed to the couple. "My mother's wish—was it a wish with a dark side or something? Or did she really make a wish that fixed everything between them? Is there some catch?"

"It has given them another chance to have a good life together," Jeannie assured Tabitha. "What they do with that is up to them, but they go into it with lessons learned."

"And Samantha and Raven?"

"As you can see, your parents changing and returning to the emotional state they were in when they met has opened the door for harmony between the Goodfellows and the Stevenses," Jeannie told me. "Your brother will...well, he gets a chance to be better than he was." Tabitha nodded. "They all have chances and new opportunities now. Choices they always had, really—but now they can understand them."

"Ok, then I know what I want," Tabitha said as she spun to face Jeannie.

"Make your first wish, then," Jeannie told her.

"I wish to wipe out the evil aspects of Michael Hayden. I want him to be a good person," Tabitha told Jeannie, and Jeannie nodded. Snapping her fingers, Michael Hayden's face relaxed as he dropped to his knees beside his sister.

My eyes narrowed.

"What?" Tabitha asked me. "You expected a larger gesture? A bigger wish? Something really earth-shattering?"

"Oh, Lord, *don't* shatter the earth," I murmured.

"For him, that's a huge thing. For Mellie, life will be better. He's her only family," Tabitha explained. "For this town? He's the most powerful fellow *in* it. Imagine what he could do if he *weren't* a selfish idiot."

I could see where she was coming from.

"Do you know what your second wish is?" Jeannie asked.

"Yes," Tabitha nodded, turning to look at the Witches Council. "I want them forced to abide by the same regulations that they lay down for everybody else."

"Wait a minute—" Mina began as she reached toward Tabitha.

"Done!" Jeannie said and snapped her fingers.

Mina's hand fixed, outstretched, a foot from Tabitha's throat.

I was silent. Shocked.

I could hear Gunther gasp behind me.

Samson snickered in my mind.

Bob was so astounded that he released his knife, and it clanked loudly on the wet floor.

Devana chuckled. Then she laughed, falling into Kyle, who reached out to hold her up. Laughter pealed from her in great sputtering bursts. As Kyle clutched the huntress, she laughed so loud and so long that her mirthful merriment echoed through the cave like a multi-layered song.

Though Mina's hand could reach no further, her eyes glittered with fury as her fingers twitched in the air.

CHAPTER 22

"This is *not* how I thought all this would end," I said to the group milling around the main room of the dorm yurt. The circuses, now nestled in the field behind my parents' shelter once again, seemed untouched by all the quiet changes that had just taken place.

"Your human friend surprised me," Gunther said. We stood in a corner together. His soft eyes watched Tabitha speaking to her parents, Samantha Goodfellow, and Raven. "Instead of taking revenge against those that wronged her, she corrected the things that led to her being wronged," he observed thoughtfully.

"I guess she skipped punishment and just went right to instantaneous rehabilitation," I told him. "Too bad everyone doesn't have just one wish. Imagine what the world would be like if everyone could fix just one big injustice or problem."

"Oh, love, even though you are skeptical and suspicious, I think you have more faith in the humans than most." Gunther brushed a hair out of my eye.

"Yeah, I know," I sighed. "Michael Hayden was not planning to buy the world a Coke with his wish."

"You know, what Tabitha did was actually smart if you think about it." Tabitha reached out and laid a hand on Bob's arm while speaking to her mother. It was an affectionate, familiar gesture, and it made me smile. "She has made them beats of a butterfly's wing."

So she had.

Michael Hayden had gathered his weeping sister in his arms and left the grotto—with our permission. He thanked Tabitha for believing in him, and he promised that he would do everything he could to live up to her faith in him. Melissa left with her legs healed and her super-strength intact. "Maybe once she heals inside, she'll be a superhero," Tabitha smiled at me as they left the grotto.

The Witches' Council disappeared as soon as Mina's limbs could move. Mina popped out first, Mabel soon after. Mercy waited, her eyes seeking mine. "They have given you a great gift," she told me from her balanced perch on a rock. "Do not abuse it."

Then she disappeared.

Everyone else came back with us to the circus so we could decompress and assess.

"Where's Uncle Phil?" Gunther asked.

"He and Jeannie left to go spend some time together."

"How'd he take it?"

"He broke into tears," I told him. We watched Kyle help Aidan walk around after he awakened from his coma. "Honestly, I think that's why they ran off alone so quickly. He didn't want anyone to see him weeping."

"We'd all understand."

"Yeah, still," I told him, and then we fell silent.

"So..." Gunther said, trailing off.

"Yeah, so..." I responded, again falling silent.

The two of you are so capable so often, and then I turn around, and you're incapacitated ninnies, Samson said to us both and hopped up on a shelf next to us. Delilah jumped up behind him and glared at us.

"I still can't get used to hearing him in my head." Gunther reached out and scratched Samson under his chin. Delilah hissed and swatted Gunther's hand away.

Hey! You have your own human! Don't you go stealing mine just because these two idiots got married! The caustic, unfamiliar female voice cracking through my brain was so shrill it made my sinuses ache.

"Dee, be nice," Gunther soothed as he petted her on the head.

I don't have to be if I don't want to be, Dee snapped. She jerked her head back and grabbed Gunther's fingers with her teeth. *You can't tell me what to do.*

Well, she's just a joy, isn't she? Samson yawned.

"Okay, enough, the two of you." I turned to face them. "Why does everyone keep claiming Gunther and I are married? He *didn't* ask, I didn't say yes, there was no wedding, no vows. What gives?"

You gave up your self-aggrandizing ringmaster superiority and invited him to have a say in what happened. You accepted, for the first time, that you are not destined to be alone. You reached out and chose to invite him to join with you. At the same time, he desperately wanted to be with you. You nincompoops did all this in the place of power. That was a merging, Samson said. *Your choices, both of you, in that moment joined the circuses.*

"Right, but—" I said, tilting my head. Delilah cut me off.

You then joined the Witches' Council, she added.

"Well, yes, but—" Gunther said. Delilah hissed and Gunther fell silent.

But nothing, blondie. That was it. Everyone joined hands and sang kumbaya, and then the human over there forced the Council to follow their own laws, the young cat said as she laid down.

You're done, Samson said.

All married, everything fixed, choices made, Delilah agreed.

"That seems anticlimactic," I said to Gunther. He looked as confused as I felt. "So we saved the world, the whole nine yards? Really?"

Well, we didn't say that, Samson said.

You could still destroy it, Delilah said.

"What do you mean?" Gunther asked her, confused.

You two are the most powerful beings in the entire world, now, Samson said. *No one can challenge you now, thanks to your human friend's wish. So what happens to the world?*

It's really up to you, Delilah said.

Congratulations, Samson said.

Slowly, Ms. Elkins' door creaked open, and the old woman shuffled out into the room slowly, her eyes burning into mine.

"I *told* you it was too soon," she rasped.

THANK YOU FOR READING!
I hope you enjoyed Hole Lotta Magic! Please think about leaving a review! Charlotte's adventures continue in Book 8, When Curse Comes to Love!

KEEP UP WITH LEANNE LEEDS

Thanks so much for reading! I hope you liked it! Want to keep up with me?

Visit leanneleeds.com to:

Find all my books…

Sign up for my newsletter…

Like me on Facebook…

Follow me on Twitter…

Follow me on Instagram…

Thanks again for reading!

Leanne Leeds

FIND A TYPO? LET US KNOW!

Typos happen. It's sad, but true.

Though we go over the manuscript multiple times, have editors, have beta readers, and advance readers it's inevitable that determined typos and mistakes sometimes find their way into a published book.

Did you find one? If you did, think about reporting it on leanneleeds.com so we can get it corrected.

www.ingramcontent.com/pod-product-compliance
Lightning Source LLC
Chambersburg PA
CBHW031610240626
47153CB00002B/700